The Quintuckles

Anita Wright

2QT Limited (Publishing)

First Edition published 2021

2QT Limited (Publishing)
Settle, North Yorkshire BD24 9BZ
www.2qt.co.uk

Cover illustration: Harriet Eyre

Printed by IngramSparks

A CIP catalogue record for this book is available
from the British Library

ISBN 978-1-914083-12-9

Dedication...

To Finley, Isla, Ella, Leo, Blake, Alice and Amaya.

...and thanks.

To Harriet Eyre for the lovely cover, to Karen Holmes, and to Catherine Cousins and her team at 2QT.

Chapter 1

Without a doubt, the Quintuckles are the most unusual family in Sprinton Avenue. As you turn into the avenue from the high street, you will notice immediately that the inhabitants of Number 35 are not like the inhabitants of any of the other houses.

All down the street, the front gardens have been stripped of their hedges and flowerbeds and laid to concrete. If your first view of the avenue is early in the morning, late in the afternoon or at the weekend, you will see a car, sometimes two cars, symmetrically parked on each of these barren plots. But there is a rebellious note in the avenue. At Number 35, the front garden has not been stripped of its greenery. A japonica hedge, tangled and thorny, encloses the small rectangular patch. A little wooden gate leads into it, and flowers and shrubs jostle within the hedge in colourful confusion.

Leaning against the shrubs, wherever there is space, are five ordinary bicycles such as you or I might ride – though these bikes all have exceptionally large baskets. You will also see a strange tandem tricycle, a small trailer and a big old-fashioned pram in the garden. Aha, you think, there is a baby living in this house! Not so – though it is true to say that this pram has bounced a good many babies in its time, including several of the occupants of the house. Nowadays the old pram is put to a very different use.

All down the avenue the front doors are meticulously painted in muted colours, reflecting the impeccable taste of the proud house owners. The front door of Number 35 is the only exception. It shows no such subtlety; it hits you in the eye.

Each of the seven occupants of the house had chosen a different colour from the paint charts. Each of them felt passionately about their choice and would not be budged. A whole week of arguing and debate failed to resolve the problem, so Ambrose had divided the door carefully into seven strips of equal width and each member of the family got busy with an individual pot of paint. The result had been a shock even to the long-suffering inhabitants of the other houses in the avenue who thought that they'd seen the worst that the Quintuckles could throw at them.

The neighbours turned their heads away in disgust whenever they had the misfortune to walk past the little gate. Seven clashing colours are certainly hard on the eyes – though the Quintuckles clearly did not think so as they got busy with their paintbrushes – but it may well have been Tallulah's virulent magenta glitter strip, so lovingly painted and only once wavering into Hannibal's emerald territory, which caused the most offence.

If you should find yourself in the avenue early in the morning on a weekday in term time, you will see most of the cars driving away, leaving their glaring patches of concrete bare and ugly. And if you hang around for long enough you will see Quentin emerging from the colourful striped door, holding his briefcase in one hand and a monocycle in the other.

He found the twisted mass of metal years ago when he was a young boy. Flung on top of a heap of rubbish left behind by the circus, it was obviously the victim of some truly awful disaster. Quentin, being but a boy and possessed of a boy's macabre imagination, liked to imagine that the damage was the result of a catastrophic acrobatic miscalculation, but I think it much more likely that the monocycle had been inadvertently run over by a careless circus vehicle.

Quentin carried it home and showed it to his father, Ambrose. Any ordinary man would have looked at the mangled bits of metal and said, 'Oh, throw it away, Quentin, that's way beyond repair.' But Ambrose, as you will discover, is no ordinary man.

Ambrose is very clever with his hands. With Quentin's

help, he took the monocycle to pieces and put it back together again with extraordinary skill. Quentin taught himself to ride it. With mind-boggling agility, he mastered the art of forward, backward and circular cycling. With both hands free, he is now a great help to Millicent, his mother, when it comes to carrying the shopping.

Now, with his briefcase tucked under his arm, he rides the monocycle to his office with no regard at all to the strange looks he gets from his neighbours. On arrival at his destination, he picks up his single wheel, carries it up the spiral staircase to his room in the roof, where he spends his days reading proofs of rather tedious documents, and stows it under the desk. So easy, don't you think? And there's not the slightest fear of it being stolen.

Soon after Quentin has left the house with his wheel, out from the dazzling door come four children in school uniform. Gertrude, Hannibal and Tallulah are the Quintuckle children. Gertrude's dark hair is short and straight, but Tallulah's hair is long and red and very curly. For school she ties it back with ribbons in plaits or bunches, but it is still very unruly. The fourth child is a friend who is staying with them and goes to school with Hannibal.

The children collect their bikes and cycle off to school. A few moments later Amaryllis, the Quintuckle children's mother, emerges with her long bright skirt

4

hitched up into a belt. She puts a pile of music books into the basket of the remaining bike, flings herself onto the saddle and pedals furiously off to a school on the other side of the town where she is the music teacher. As well as teaching music, Amaryllis is a quite outstanding pianist, as well as being a dulcimer player. She is much in demand for concerts in the locality.

This leaves the trailer, the tandem tricycle and the pram outside the house, and Ambrose and Millicent inside the house. The trailer, the tandem and the pram will not be needed until Saturday morning. Ambrose and Millicent, on the other hand, are needed every day for the domestic running of the household.

On most days, after the breakfast dishes have been cleared away and washed, the beds made and a modicum of housework done, Millicent and Ambrose get down to more serious business. Millicent climbs up to the attic where she will spend the morning blowing her clarinet and tinkering with her drums, and Ambrose descends to his workshop in the semi-basement.

Ambrose makes dulcimers, not the more common hammer dulcimer but the beautifully strung graceful instruments with a pleasing timbre. He is a wonderful craftsman.

Amaryllis plays the dulcimer, and it was when she came to choose one of Ambrose's exquisite instruments for her twenty-first birthday that she met Quentin. He was just riding out of the gate on his monocycle when she arrived, and her first impression was not 'how very interesting!' but 'how very odd!' Quentin is tall and thin, and on his monocycle he looks more like a cartoon character than a real person. Little did Amaryllis guess then that she would end up married to him and living at Number 35.

Subsequent visits to Ambrose's workshop confirmed her opinion that Quentin was indeed exceedingly eccentric but, fortunately for the future existence of Gertrude, Hannibal and Tallulah, she also found him more and more endearing. For his part, Quentin loved the beautiful, raven-haired Amaryllis from the moment he saw her. He had nearly fallen off his wheel and only stopped wobbling when he turned out of the avenue.

Ambrose remains absorbed in his work, only vaguely aware of the rhythmic reverberations from the heights of the house, until he hears Millicent calling him for their bread and cheese lunch. After lunch and a little nap, Ambrose and Millicent will go together to the attic where they will go bananas in a jam session. Ambrose will not, as you might imagine, play the dulcimer – though he is a tolerably good player. No, Ambrose also plays the xylophone and is a mighty master of the trumpet, and Millicent is an ace drummer.

Can you even begin to imagine the extent of the noise that he and Millicent make together? Fortunately, at this time of the day there is no one in at Number 37 to which Number 35 is attached. By the end of the session, much

6

of Millicent's grey hair has escaped its hairpins and is tumbling joyfully down her back. Such hair as Ambrose has is all in place, but the bald part of his pate has a fine sheen.

So much for the weekdays. But this story begins on a Saturday, and on Saturdays the pattern of events in Sprinton Avenue is very different.

On this particular Saturday, the weather was wonderful; it was a fine sunny morning in late July. Soon the school holidays would begin. Gertrude, who was thirteen at the time, and Hannibal, who was twelve, were already attending their senior school. Tallulah was ten and about to start her final year in the primary school. There was no school friend staying with them at that time.

Many of the concreted front gardens were showing signs of activity. Cars were being carefully washed and waxed and polished, front doorsteps were being scrubbed, and small children were being told to get out of the way.

The Quintuckles, too, were active. Hannibal was in the little front garden, just finishing mending a puncture in the back tyre of his bike. His flute and his saxophone were already stowed in his large saddlebag. Like his grandfather and his father, Hannibal was very good with mechanical things. He could mend almost anything, and he loved a challenge. He seemed to have an inborn knowledge of how mechanical things worked – a very useful ability to have, I'm sure that you will agree.

Amaryllis, her dulcimer strapped to her back, appeared from the striped door. She was struggling with one of Millicent's drums. Behind her came Quentin and Millicent. Between them they had the rest of the drum kit and the xylophone. They loaded their burdens into the pram. The springs, twanging only slightly, adjusted themselves easily to the strain – people knew how to make prams in the far-off days when this one was constructed.

Ambrose came out next and added his trumpet and Millicent's clarinet to the pram. He gathered up the tandem tricycle and, by means of an attachment of his own devising, fastened the pram to the back of it. He and Millicent manoeuvred their vehicle out of the gate and waited by the kerb.

Quentin had gone back into the house. Amaryllis was attaching the trailer to her bicycle and shouting at the children. 'Hurry up, you lot. Ambrose and Millicent are ready and waiting.' Her voice was clear and musical and carried a long way.

Hannibal pushed his bike out of the gate as Gertrude, with her cello, and Tallulah, with her oboe, came out of the rainbow door. Tallulah plays the violin too, but not on Saturday mornings. Gertrude is quite a good pianist, but on the cello, she is truly remarkable. Her cello fits neatly into the trailer.

Gertrude's hair, gypsy-black like her mother's, was

neatly held back with a blue ribbon. Hannibal, for some reason known only to himself, had spiked his dark hair echidna style. As this was not a school day, Tallulah had neglected to do anything at all with her long, tangled, auburn locks. All the children were dressed in a bizarre, but not unbecoming, collection of garments. Amaryllis has a fine eye when it comes to charity-shop bargains.

Gertrude, Hannibal and Tallulah love Saturdays. Gertrude was planning to go riding that afternoon – she adores horses. Occasionally Quentin goes with her. He used to ride a lot when he was a boy and still likes to ride when he gets the chance. Hannibal planned to join his football team for training or a match, and Tallulah was looking forward to her dance class.

Then Quentin emerged with a double bass, which he strapped carefully into the trailer. 'Only your trombone to come now,' he said cheerfully to Amaryllis. He popped back through the door, soon to reappear with a bright-red trombone case. The dulcimer is a very quiet instrument, and the gentle sound can get lost in a busy street. Sometimes Amaryllis needs to play something with a bit more bite. As you will appreciate, the trombone is hugely generous with its bite.

Quentin locked the door and soon they were all away, pedalling up the avenue. Ambrose, Gertrude, Hannibal and Tallulah were in the lead on their bicycles; Amaryllis was behind them, standing up on her pedals to get a bit of pressure to help her tow the trailer. Millicent was next on the tricycle-pram combination, and Quentin was bringing up the rear on his monocycle, his legs circling merrily, and the trombone safely cradled in his arms.

They called out friendly greetings to their car-cleaning neighbours, greetings which were returned rather reluctantly. There was much shaking of heads and tut-tutting after the convoy had passed. The Quintuckles were considered to be decidedly odd, not at all suitable residents for the respectable houses in the road. Yet many of the wives and children, who were currently getting ready to go into town for the weekend's shopping, would be more than happy to encounter their much-maligned neighbours later on that morning.

On this, the last Saturday of the summer term, the Quintuckles were under the impression that this was to be a Saturday like any other. They were in for a shock.

Chapter 2

Once out of the avenue and heading down the high street towards the town centre, the Quintuckles were greeted with waves and cries of, 'Looking forward to hearing you later!' Outside the avenue they are very popular. Those residents of Windleford who do not have to live near the Quintuckles regard them as a town treasure.

A large leafy square at the end of the high street is the attractive focus of the little town of Windleford. The main shopping streets lead out of it, but the square itself is a quiet traffic-free haven, a perfect place for playing music. The tall buildings enclosing it make for excellent acoustics, and it was here that the Quintuckles stopped, unloaded their instruments and tuned up.

The benches scattered around the square were already filling up with eager regulars and, as the first notes resonated over the town, other listeners were quickly drawn in. It must be said that quite a few residents of Sprinton Avenue were among the crowd; they ceased to be stuffy when they were away from the avenue and in the town square.

On this Saturday, as on any other, the Quintuckles switched smoothly from one tune to another. Swing, rock, jazz and classical music poured out in seemingly effortless profusion. Millicent's arms were moving so fast that it is a wonder they didn't fly off her body. All the Quintuckles were completely at one with their instruments and communicated with nods and winks and smiles. Occasionally one of them took a solo spot, giving the others a brief respite.

The square soon filled to overflowing with entranced, toe-tapping listeners. Children – and even a few uninhibited adults – were dancing as usual. Two policemen, standing on the periphery, were tapping their toes and grinning rather inanely. There was a time when they had tried to move on the Quintuckles, but they'd given that up long ago and decided to turn their backs on legality and enjoy the music instead.

Over the music a loud voice from the crowd rang out. 'Hey, Tallulah, when are *you* going to bang the drums?'

Millicent smiled and slowed the beat, keeping it going with one stick and holding the other out to Tallulah. Tallulah faded out her phrase on the oboe and crossed to the drums. Without losing the rhythm, she took the other drumstick. The others gradually stopped playing as Millicent handed the second stick to Tallulah.

Now Tallulah was alone on the drums. She is an excellent oboe player, brilliant for her age, but on the drums she is absolutely ace. She is small, but wiry and strong. The sticks hammered away at the drums in a frenzy of rhythm. The applause was, as always, deafening.

Throughout the morning, there was a steady clinking noise and sometimes even the sound of rustling in the vicinity of Amaryllis's open trombone case. The Quintuckles never ask for money; they play for the enjoyment of themselves and others. Nevertheless, the money comes in useful to ensure tip-top maintenance for their instruments and to secure weekly visits to London for the children's – strictly classical – music lessons.

Several hours later, after repeated encores, the Quintuckles were played out and the instruments were packed away. The cycle convoy headed back towards Number 35 Sprinton Avenue and a well-earned lunch. Mouths were already watering. Amaryllis was responsible for the weekend cooking and there was an Amaryllis special waiting in the oven.

So far things were normal for a fine Saturday morning. But not for long.

The little cavalcade turned off the high street onto Sprinton Avenue. A van with a box trailer was parked untidily a little way down the avenue. 'Hello!' said Ambrose. 'Someone's getting a delivery. Another new sofa for Number 12, perhaps!'

But Hannibal, cycling in front, had spotted something rather surprising for Sprinton Avenue: a masked face was peering round the van. He leapt off his bike in excitement. Tallulah cycled into him and fell off. The others jammed on their brakes and juddered to a standstill. The drums growled, reverberating in protest.

'Look sharp!' Hannibal said. 'They must be going to rob a bank. Watch carefully – we'll be required as witnesses. There's no one but us around.'

Gertrude regarded him loftily. 'Don't be silly, Hann. There isn't a bank anywhere near here.'

Hardly were the words out of her mouth when two men wearing the uniforms of security guards and, alarmingly, also masked, jumped out of the van and lowered a ramp from the box trailer. They were joined by the other man in a mask. All three raced towards the Quintuckles, who had come to a standstill with their mouths open in amazement.

Such confusion followed that later the Quintuckles were unable to untangle the order of events. A fluster of wheels and a grabbing of musicians, and somehow all the musical instruments and the entire family of Quintuckles were bundled into the box trailer. After them went the monocycle and the tricycle – it was a very big trailer! The bikes, the Quintuckle trailer and the pram were left behind, thrown down haphazardly at the side of the road.

Somewhere in the middle of it all the Quintuckles heard a voice calling out, 'Hey, what's going on?'

There was a reply in a loud, grating voice. 'Don't worry, madam. We're arresting these people for public nuisance offences.'

'Well, I can't say I'm surprised. I saw the police at the Quintuckle house this morning. I guessed something was up!' They recognised the voice of Mrs Green who lived at Number 30, almost opposite Number 35. She was always complaining about the Quintuckles. She was certainly going to enjoy spreading this latest Quintuckle story up and down the road!

The back of the trailer was clanged shut and the Quintuckles heard bolts being drawn across. It was dark inside and very cramped. It was a big trailer, but it now had a lot of people and a great deal of stuff inside it. There was no window, although a crack of light showed through the ill-fitting doors.

With a horrible grinding of gears and a jolt, which threw the Quintuckles and their instruments into an even more tangled jumble, the van took off down Sprinton Avenue at a rate well above the designated speed limit, the trailer bouncing along behind it.

For a few startled moments, the Quintuckles were

thrown into such a state of turmoil that they were uncharacteristically silent, but then there was a sudden babble as they regained their voices.

'This is ridiculous!'

'What on earth…!'

'Get off my head, you idiot.' Tallulah's voice was muffled.

'We've been arrested.'

'Don't be silly. Masked men don't arrest people. Policemen do the arresting!'

'Well, what was all that about the police going into our house this morning? Why on earth would the police be remotely interested in *our* house?'

'Perhaps they saw some suspicious characters around it.'

'I don't think we've been *arrested*. I think we've been kidnapped' said Quentin grimly.

'But who on earth would want to kidnap us?' demanded Hannibal. 'Could someone please untangle me from this drum?'

'Where's my dulcimer?'

'My leg's stuck.'

'Where are the bikes?'

'What about the trailer?'

'And the pram!'

Millicent's voice cut through the babble. 'Let's just stop and sort ourselves out, then perhaps we'll be able to think straight.'

With much grunting and heaving, they extricated themselves from each other and their musical appendages and sat on the floor of the trailer, protecting themselves as far as possible from the sliding instruments and the excruciatingly uncomfortable bumps of the wheels. There was the faintest crack of light coming in round the edges of the doors at the back of the trailer. As their eyes adjusted, they could see that there were long, lidded boxes along the sides of the space. At least that provided them with somewhere to sit!

'What now? What on earth do we do now?' Millicent's question hung quivering in the air.

No one had the *slightest* idea what to do.

'I hope the lunch won't be spoiled.'

Ambrose's remark was greeted by a groan of despair. After the exertions of the morning, they were all ravenously hungry.

Quentin fought his way to the front of the trailer and started banging on it. 'Let us out, you idiots!' he yelled.

The others joined in. 'Let us out!'

Amaryllis had an idea and tried to get everyone's attention but, try as she might, she simply couldn't make herself heard. She scrabbled around on the floor and managed to locate her trombone. She put it to her lips and blew. The slide hit Hannibal on the nose, and the blast of noise from the trombone and the outraged shout of pain from Hannibal combined to cut through the cacophony of yells.

In the resulting silence Amaryllis spoke. 'That's not nearly enough noise,' she said. 'We need to make much more of a racket. We need people outside to hear and complain to the police. Come on, find your instruments and blow and scrape and bang for all you're worth.'

The ensuing noise was deafening, and the trailer began to rock alarmingly with their vigorous movement and the incredible din. Unfortunately for the Quintuckles, the van and trailer were by this time well into the country. The only person to hear the hubbub was a farmer herding cows into a field, and his only response was to shake his fist and swear.

Eventually sheer exhaustion forced the Quintuckles to quieten down.

'What now?' asked Gertrude.

'There's a wider crack at the top of the door. Climb on my shoulders, Hannibal,' said Quentin. 'Can you see where we are?'

Hannibal clambered onto his father's shoulders and put his eye to the tiny slit of light. 'Just fields and hedges – that's all I can see. I don't recognise anything. I don't have a clue where we are. Not a house in sight. It looks like the middle of nowhere.'

They looked despairingly at each other in the gloom and gave themselves up to the discomfort of the wheels. Even so, they did their best to protect their instruments from the worst of the shaking and rattling; musical instruments are too precious to be abandoned to circumstance.

The van and the trailer went on and on, on and on.

Suddenly there was a squeal of brakes. The Quintuckles' torpor was shaken by the most enormous bump as the trailer came to a standstill. There was a lot of shouting outside, but they couldn't make out any words. They waited in silence. They were usually a pretty brave lot, but at that moment they were all mightily afraid.

What would happen now? Surely the doors would open. But the doors did not open. There was no friendly light, just a lot of clanging and shouting.

'Unhitch the trailer now!'

'Okay, trailer unhitched!'

'Start the winch!'

There was a clanging of chains being dragged and the sound of metal against metal. The trailer was jolted sharply and seemed to be being dragged uphill.

Hannibal, who had clambered over boxes to try to see through the high-up slit, suddenly fell over and sprawled onto the floor of the trailer. In the dimness, Tallulah tripped over him. They were both too exhausted to argue and they just lay there in utter despair.

The trailer came to a standstill and the Quintuckles heard the sound of an engine fading away. The van that had drawn the trailer was leaving. There was a loud clang, as of a metal door closing. The little slit of light vanished and the Quintuckles were now in total darkness.

Ambrose was enraged. 'They've locked us into

something.'

Tallulah had had enough. She began to wail. 'They've driven us into one of those container lorries. There won't be any air. We'll die in here.'

'Don't be so melodramatic, Tallulah. There's some air coming in through that little slit at the top of the door.' Amaryllis tried to sound calm, but her voice was sharp with anxiety. Visions of her family expiring through lack of oxygen floated before her. She reached into the darkness. Her fingers found Tallulah's mop of curls and she drew her daughter to her, hugging her fiercely. Amazingly, Tallulah didn't fight her off.

The Quintuckles were utterly bewildered; they had not the remotest idea what to do. Hannibal extricated himself from an assortment of arms and legs and started banging on the sides of the trailer again. 'Let us out!' he shouted. 'You can't leave us here to die!'

'Do be quiet, Hann,' said Quentin. 'I can't hear myself think. I'm working on a plan.'

Hannibal slumped back onto the floor of the trailer. 'Well then, hurry up and think of a plan that will work before we all die of hunger as well as lack of air.'

'Typical! Trust you to think of your stomach when we're all in mortal danger!' Gertrude jabbed her elbow into what she thought was Hannibal's ribs but was in fact her grandfather's back.

'Hey, watch out! That hurt!' Ambrose yelled.

'What on earth is going on? Aren't things bad enough

already?' Millicent sounded exasperated.

And suddenly, their nerves on edge, they were all shouting at each other.

Another great clang silenced them and then there was a sudden roar, an engine undoubtedly. And now they were moving again, bumping at a furious speed. Family and instruments slithered around. Tallulah was torn from Amaryllis's grip and found herself crammed up in a corner. She curled up in a ball with her arms over her head and prayed to wake up. She must be dreaming. There could be no other explanation.

The bumping ceased abruptly. It was followed by a strange sensation of floating as the engine changed tune. Gertrude, who is susceptible to pressure, moaned and pressed her hands over her ears. The noise of the engine diminished to a steady growl. Things stopped sliding around.

'Good heavens!' said Ambrose. 'I do believe we're in an aeroplane! We've taken off! We're in some sort of transport plane. We're flying!'

'Don't be silly, Ambrose,' said Millicent. 'That's impossible!'

'I rather fear that Ambrose may be right,' said Quentin grimly.

Chapter 3

The Quintuckles fell silent. All there was now was a steady engine hum, darkness and a tangle of people and musical instruments.

And then they heard a sound: someone was moving about outside the trailer. They heard banging and scraping, and a light was turned on in the roof. It was quite a harsh light; after the thick darkness, it made the Quintuckle family gasp and screw up their eyes.

The light revealed the extent of the disarray into which the family and their instruments had been thrown. Their first thought was to ensure that the trumpet, the dulcimer, the trombone, the oboe, the flute, the saxophone, the clarinet, the double bass, the cello, the drums and the xylophone were all unharmed. The Quintuckles scrabbled around and gathered them all up. There was a cacophony of blowing and twanging, of scraping and banging, followed by a universal sigh of relief when they realised that the instruments had suffered nothing worse than a few surface scratches.

Now they turned their attention to themselves. They were all in a highly dishevelled state, with hair tangled and clothes rumpled as if they had been dragged through the proverbial hedge not only backwards but forwards and sideways as well. Millicent's hair, completely devoid of grips, was all over the place. The floor of the trailer was not particularly clean, and hands and faces were streaked with dirt. They looked – and felt – a very sorry lot indeed.

Then they heard a voice, a man's voice, the same voice that had spoken to the woman in Sprinton Avenue but not so threatening now. In fact, it sounded quite kind and almost jolly. It came from a hidden loudspeaker somewhere above their heads.

'Please place all your instruments in the boxes provided. This is for their safety.'

'A bit late to think about that,' muttered Ambrose.

'And what about our safety, I'd like to know?' yelled Hannibal.

'You will also find food.' The voice was commanding, insistent, but not at all harsh.

'I suppose they've got us where they want us now, so they don't have to be so beastly to us,' muttered Millicent.

'You will also find cushions and blankets for your comfort,' the voice continued.

'Comfort!' snorted Hannibal. 'Not much chance of that!'

'What about some air?' shouted Quentin.

'Don't worry. The air conditioning is coming on now.'

'Well, that's a relief,' muttered Amaryllis.

The Quintuckles started opening the boxes that were piled at the sides of the trailer. One of them was full of sheet music and books. It was their own music! Their captors must have collected up every bit of music in the house – classical and jazz, folk music, popular songs, old songs, and so on and so on. But most of the boxes were empty and there was plenty of room for the instruments, even for the double bass and the drum kit and the xylophone. Soon everything was carefully and securely stowed away, leaving quite a lot more space for the family.

One of the boxes that was not empty yielded a pleasant surprise. Food! Plenty of it, and extraordinarily delicious. It was food that was rarely seen in the Quintuckle household: succulent ham; smoked salmon; cheese; grapes; Florentines; chocolate truffles, and exotic tropical fruits.

Far from taking away their hunger, the combination of fear and fury had sharpened the Quintuckles' appetites. They fell upon the food with enthusiasm, though Tallulah was heard to mutter that the 'Amaryllis special' in the oven would have been far nicer and would by now be burnt to a cinder.

Amaryllis assured her that the oven was on a timer and would switch itself off. The food would not be burnt.

'But what's the good of that? We'll never get to eat it,' wailed Tallulah. 'We must be hundreds of miles away from home. I wish something good would happen!'

There was silence for a moment then Amaryllis said, 'I can think of something good.'

'What?' they all spoke in chorus.

'We're all together. Just think how awful it would have been if some of us had not gone to the square today. They would have been left behind, with no idea of where we had disappeared to!' They all agreed that indeed, that would have been awful.

At that moment, the lights were extinguished with startling suddenness and the Quintuckles were once more plunged into darkness. After an initial babble of dismay, they fell silent.

'Does everyone have a cushion and blanket?' asked Amaryllis.

With no light, they felt for the cushions and blankets that they had tipped out of the boxes in order to make room for the instruments. There was much confusion as they sorted them out, then they all fell silent as the plane droned on and on, heading for who knows where. Replete with food, and exhausted from their musical exertions and the trauma of being kidnapped, one after another the Quintuckles, with the exception of Millicent, eventually drifted off into a state of semi-sleep.

Millicent remained wide awake, her brain in overdrive. She was a great sorter out of problems. Now she went over the events of the last few hours in detail. She must protect her family somehow; there surely must be something she could do. But it was no good. Although Millicent did an enormous amount of thinking, she could make no sense of it at all. The sequence of events went round and round inside her head, but no solution presented itself. Eventually she closed her eyes; maybe if she gave her brain a rest, she would be able to think straight.

The plane droned on and on. The Quintuckles twitched and muttered in their half sleep. Hours passed, but eventually they were stirred into complete wakefulness when the engine noise changed. Gertrude moaned again, her hands cradling her ears. They felt the vibrations of the landing gear unfolding.

'What now?' asked Quentin. 'It seems that we have arrived somewhere – but where?'

They waited for something to happen, but no doors opened, no lights came on. The darkness remained complete. After a short time, the engine noise started up and they felt the plane taking off once more.

'It was just a refuelling stop,' said Ambrose when they were airborne again. 'We must be going a very long way.'

The Quintuckles drifted back into their semi-sleep,

but there was a good deal of mutinous muttering and grumbling. And the plane flew on, and on and on.

Several hours later, the Quintuckles were again startled into full wakefulness by the rattle of the landing gear. Soon they felt the plane touch down – and now the van was flooded with blinding light.

They looked at each other with dismay. What a mess they all were! And what a pickle they were in – incredibly dishevelled, with their clothes all awry. Millicent had lost all her hairpins, and her long hair fell around her shoulders in an untidy grey cloud. Gertrude and Tallulah looked exceedingly shaggy. Only Amaryllis, with her helmet of dark hair cut close to her head, looked reasonably neat. Ambrose, Quentin and Hannibal resembled bristly brushes.

Quentin looked at his watch. A quick calculation informed him that it was more than twenty-three hours since they had been bundled into the van on their way home from their music making in the square. He reckoned that must have been at about half past five in the afternoon. Where on earth were they now? A very long way from home, that was clear!

They had missed their usual Sunday morning slot in the church Family Service and the congregation must be wondering what had happened to them. By now, they should be in the middle of their Sunday afternoon session at the Sunnyside Café. No doubt their telephone had been ringing to enquire about their whereabouts.

Quentin wondered what people were thinking about their disappearance – and whether anything was being done about it. Maybe people had just shrugged their shoulders and said, 'Oh well, that's the Quintuckles for you! Typical! You never know what they'll get up to next!'

But there was no time to think about that now. There was a great deal of clanking and banging from outside, then all the Quintuckles suddenly toppled over and landed in a heap as the van dropped and landed on solid ground. There was a moment of stunned silence before they heard men shouting outside and the rattle of a key turning in the lock of the van door.

The door of the van groaned opened. The Quintuckles took a deep breath of welcome fresh air, staggered to their feet and rushed towards it.

Outside it was dark, but it was a darkness pierced with a full moon and thousands of stars. They gazed in awe at the great arc of moonlight and starlight above them.

'Good heavens!' said Quentin. 'It must be Sunday teatime at home but it's night-time here. We've certainly come a very long way. We must be on the other side of the world! And that means that we've gone back in time. We are in yesterday! And this doesn't seem to be an airport. There are no other planes that I can see. It's just a private strip!'

Another moment of stunned silence and then Tallulah muttered, 'Yesterday? How did we manage to get into yesterday?' Then they all began to speak at once. There was such a babble of noise that it was hard to make sense of anything.

Chapter 4

The men who had seemed so threatening in Sprinton
Avenue were now slapping each other on the back.
There were five of them, all laughing and talking loudly.
One of them detached himself from the group and came
towards the Quintuckles.

'Welcome to our island!' he said. They recognised his
voice as the one which had given the instructions about
stowing away the instruments in the boxes and had told
them where to find food. 'I'm sure you will be happy
here.' He didn't sound at all harsh, nor aggressive, nor so
menacing as he had done through the loudspeaker on the
plane. In fact, he sounded really friendly and pleasant.

'I'm Luke,' he said and held out his hand to Quentin.
'And you, I know, are Quentin – and I know all your names
too,' he added, smiling at the huddle of Quintuckles.

The four other men who had seemed so terrifying in

Sprinton Avenue came towards the Quintuckles with broad grins on their faces. They seemed friendly and eager to shake hands. The Quintuckles were confused. They took the proffered hands and shook them politely, while Luke announced their names: Ed, Phil, Joel and Jack.

But why were the kidnappers being so friendly after abducting the Quintuckles so violently? They had acted in such an aggressive and ferocious manner but now they were being so welcoming and polite. It didn't make any sort of sense at all.

'Where are we?' demanded Ambrose. 'And why have you brought us here?'

The only reply was a broad smile.

Gertrude thought she had the answer. 'We're being held hostage,' she said. 'Don't you see? We are valuable until they get their money, so they have to be nice to us! And then, when they have the money, if we're lucky they'll take us back home and hope that we'll tell everyone how kind they were so that no one will go searching for them in order to punish them.'

'If that is the case, we'll never get home. We have no rich relatives or friends to pay the ransom,' said Quentin.

The group of men looked at each other, shaking their heads and laughing.

'Where are we, and why have you brought us here?' demanded Ambrose again.

'You are not hostages, I assure you. This is nothing to

do with money. This is to do with your talents! Follow me, please.' Luke led them towards a large wooden structure at the edge of the field.

'What are you going to do with our instruments?' demanded Quentin.

'Don't worry, they will be quite safe. We are quite aware that you need them.'

The Quintuckles followed Luke, and the other four men followed behind. No one said a word. The silence was eventually broken by Ambrose who, as they entered a large wooden cabin at the edge of the field, sighed deeply and muttered, '"O Time, thou must unravel this, not I. It is too hard a knot for me to untie."' Ambrose reckons that Shakespeare has a word for everything, and he is probably right!

From the outside, the building seemed ordinary enough. It looked like an extremely large wooden garden shed. But inside it was quite astonishing. It was just one large room, beautifully furnished with carpets, comfortable chairs and elegant little tables. There was even a grand piano, to which Amaryllis was immediately drawn. The Quintuckles all play the piano with varying degrees of competence, but Amaryllis is the queen bee.

She stood at the piano and ran her fingers over the keys. Ripples of music floated around the room. Every head turned to look at her. 'This is a strange place for a piano,' she said. 'But it's wonderfully in tune! I'm amazed! Who looks after it?'

'A friend of Sir Wally's from his schooldays. You will like him, I'm sure,' said Luke. 'He comes here every now and then to have a holiday – and to tune the piano, of course! The piano is here because we use this cabin as a meeting place for the islanders. It's a sort of village hall. We have birthday parties, exchange fruit and vegetables and plants, that sort of thing. Everyone loves it when Paul Simmons comes out here. He can play the hymns for us on Sundays, otherwise our unaccompanied singing is somewhat ragged.'

Amaryllis stared at him. 'Paul Simmons? But I know him! I used to know him very well indeed. He was a piano student of mine a few years ago. He was such a talented pianist and had a particularly good ear. He didn't want the concert platform life, though. He hates playing in public, so he decided to train as a piano tuner. But he moved away from Windleford and I haven't heard anything of him lately. Did he marry, I wonder? He had a very nice girlfriend.'

Luke grinned and said, 'Yes, he did marry. I think you'll find that Paul and Sally will be visiting very soon and bringing their baby with them. It was Paul who told us about your family and your wonderful music. He will be surprised to find you here!'

There was a long silence as the Quintuckles absorbed this information. So that was how this Sir Wally had heard about them. An innocent remark by Paul to an old school friend had led to the kidnapping of the entire

Quintuckle family!

'Well, I must say life suddenly seems to be full of surprises,' said Amaryllis eventually. She sat down on the piano stool and started to play a Schumann Arabesque. The Quintuckles and kidnappers all sat down together and listened as the music rose and fell, swelling and waning. Then Amaryllis switched from Schumann to Chopin and it was as if a strong spell had been cast. Everyone within range was captivated, entranced.

Amaryllis finished playing. She sat quietly at the piano, her hands in her lap. There was silence in the room for a moment – a silence broken by a torrent of clapping. As the clapping faded, the clip-clop of horses' hooves was heard approaching outside.

The clip-clopping got louder and then faded away as the horses passed by. All the men in the building, with the exception of Luke, heaved themselves out of their chairs and went out of the shed. Luke and the Quintuckles sat on in silence. Then there was the sound of hooves again; here came the horses, returning from wherever they had been. They passed by the building and the sound faded.

'Well,' said Luke, 'I must say I did enjoy the music – very uplifting. I'm beginning to see the sense of getting you all here. I thought the boss was crazy sending us off to England to collect you, but he was absolutely insistent that you must come. It was quite a complicated business, you know. It's bad enough abducting one person, but a whole family! Plus a collection of musical instruments! That is an altogether more complex procedure and a lot of planning was needed. But I'm beginning to see why it was worth all the difficulty. You will be collected soon. Meanwhile, make yourselves comfortable whilst we wait.'

You might think that this would have been the cue for the Quintuckles to bombard Luke with questions, to try to sort out just what was happening to them, but they were too exhausted. The chairs were indeed comfortable – exceedingly comfortable. The room was warm. They were tired and, one by one, they fell into a deep sleep.

Chapter 5

The sleepers were awoken by the sound of horses again and Luke's voice. 'Time to go now. Your transport is here. Come along. We'll take you to your new home where you may sleep for as long as you like. Tomorrow you will meet Sir Wally.'

'And who might Sir Wally be?' asked Quentin.

'Sir Walter. He is the owner of this island.'

There was a chorus of questions from the Quintuckles.

'What island? What is the island called?'

'Where exactly in the world are we?'

'Why have you kidnapped us?'

'How long are you going to keep us here?'

And a long wail from Tallulah, 'I want to go home.'

'The horses are waiting,' Luke said. 'Come along – and don't worry. All your questions will be answered in time. You'll soon get used to being here, and I'm sure you will love it.'

'Horses?' said Gertrude. 'I love horses.'

'I'm hungry,' wailed Hannibal.

'Well, that's nothing new,' said Tallulah. 'You're always hungry.'

'Don't worry. There's plenty of food in your cabin. Come along!' urged Luke.

The Quintuckles were herded out of the front of the building. Outside was a large cart pulled by two very big horses.

'Wow!' said Tallulah. 'Fantastic! I've never travelled by horse and cart before.'

'What beautiful horses,' said Gertrude. 'They're draught horses, aren't they? What sort? And what are their names.'

'They are Percherons. The bigger one is George, and this one is Bess,' replied the large man who was holding their reins. 'Best draught horses in the world. Wonderful for pulling heavy loads. We've needed the big wagon today to transport all your stuff to your cabin. Our other horses are a more normal size, and you'll easily manage them. Up you get, all of you. In my opinion, this is the best way to travel by far! You'll soon get used to it. We have no motor vehicles on the island, with the exception of a couple of tractors. Cars wouldn't last long on our tracks! We rely on our horses and our bikes. Welcome to the island. I like a bit of music and I'm looking forward to your concerts. I'm Robin, by the way. We've been told your names, of course, and I'll try and learn which one is which as we go along.'

'Up you all get,' said Luke. 'Robin is in charge of all the horses. You're lucky to get him today because he is mostly up at the stables.'

The Quintuckles clambered into the cart and Luke got in after them. The seats were along the sides, leaving plenty of space in the middle.

They had given up asking questions. Bewildered by all that had happened to them in the past few hours, they were becoming resigned to the fact that life had ceased to be normal. Most of them were secretly thinking – and hoping – that they must be having a wild dream, and at any minute they would wake up.

For about twenty minutes they bumped along the rough track. Every now and then, they passed a log cabin. Some had lit windows, and some were in darkness. Once, a door opened and someone shouted a friendly greeting to which Luke responded, 'Hello! The new arrivals. Off to their cabin!'

'Great! Hi there, all of you! I'm really looking forward to your music and to getting to know you all,' was the response.

A few minutes later, the horses were pulled up with a 'Whoa there!' and soon Robin and Luke were helping the Quintuckles to clamber down from the cart.

Robin said, 'Cheerio, Quintuckles. See you soon, no doubt. What about you, Luke? Are you staying here or coming on with me? I need to deliver something to Sir Wally.'

'Could you wait for me, Robin? I need to see Sir Wally, too. I'll just introduce this new family of ours to their new home. I won't be long.'

The Quintuckles found themselves outside what looked, in the moonlight, like an extremely large ranch – a long single-storey building made of wood but very much bigger than any other log cabin they had seen. There were welcoming lights on inside.

'Oh, listen!' said Gertrude. 'We must be very near the sea! I can hear the surf.'

There was a huge door knocker on the heavy wooden door. It was a carving of a treble clef, beautifully done. 'Someone on the island is a clever woodworker,' said Quentin as he lifted the knocker and tried an experimental tap on the door. 'Knock knock knock. Who's there?' he muttered.

The treble-clef carving was attached to a thin slab of rock which banged against another slab of rock that was attached to the door. The resulting sound was thunderous. There would certainly be no difficulty in hearing visitors!

The Quintuckles opened the door and walked in. They found themselves in a huge entrance hall furnished with a large dresser, a coat rack with plenty of hooks, several small tables, armchairs, a box of tennis racquets and an enormous bookcase absolutely full of books. In the centre of the room was a large table, in the middle of which was a bowl of colourful exotic-looking flowers and a big brass bell.

Millicent crossed to the table and buried her nose in the flowers. 'Mmmm,' she said. 'Wonderful!' and she flopped down into one of the big armchairs.

Hannibal crossed to the table and picked up the bell. He rang it; it had an excessively loud ring.

'Goodness gracious!' exclaimed Amaryllis as she covered her ears. 'Stop it, for heaven's sake, Hann. That is enough racket to wake the dead!'

'I'm sure that you'll find that very useful.' Luke was laughing. 'The sound carries a long way. It might save a lot of hunting for wandering children!'

At the far end of this enormous room was a huge window through which they could see the moon shining onto a great expanse of moving water. The house seemed to be perched on a cliff high above the sea. To the right of the window was a door. They all had the same thought: there must be a path leading from outside that door and descending to the sea below.

'I'm going to let you settle in now,' said Luke. 'You will no doubt want to explore your new home and sort out your rooms. I'll be back in the morning to show you around, and then I will introduce you to Sir Walter.'

'Just a moment, Luke,' said Ambrose. 'Before you go, could you tell us a little about this "Sir Walter"? Who exactly is he – and why are we here? I really do think that we deserve an explanation of some sort.'

'Sir Walter will explain things himself,' said Luke. 'He is in charge and he will tell you all you want to know. It was he who sent us to fetch you. Don't worry, everything will be made clear. No more explanations tonight. Sir Walter wishes to talk to you. By the way, unless we are being formal for some reason, we call him "Sir Wally" or even just "Wally"! He doesn't stand on ceremony. Good night. Sleep well.' And he turned to go.

'Wait a minute,' said Amaryllis. 'Where are our musical instruments?'

'Don't worry, I assure you that they are all quite safe. Sir Wally was very adamant that your instruments should be well looked after. He is looking forward to your concerts – as are all the rest of us. Take a look around. You'll soon find your things. You won't find the pram, or the trailer, or the tricycle, or the monocycle but they will arrive tomorrow.'

And he turned and went out into the moonlit night. The Quintuckles followed him to the door and watched him climb up beside Robin. Robin cried, 'Giddy up,' to the horses and Luke shouted, 'Goodbye! I'll see you in the morning!' and then they were gone.

The creaking of the wagon and the clop of the horses' hooves faded away. For a long moment, the Quintuckles all stood absolutely still. No one spoke until Hannibal suddenly broke the silence. 'Well, this is a bit of an adventure!' he said, walking back into the cabin with the others following him. 'It's certainly a far cry from Sprinton Avenue!' Suddenly he started to laugh. That set them all off, and soon they were all laughing hysterically and wiping the tears from their eyes.

Quentin brought up the rear and closed the door behind him. 'I see there is no key,' he said. 'We'll just have to trust that there are no intruders on this strange and faraway island! Well, let's explore! I really do think that I am dreaming, but let the dream continue! Whatever will happen next, I wonder? It would seem that we are on some sort of concert tour – though the strangest concert tour ever! Let's see if we can sort out our rooms.'

'I'm hungry!' announced Hannibal. 'I vote that we start our exploration in the kitchen and see if there's anything to eat.'

'You're always hungry. What about all that food we had on the plane?' asked Tallulah.

'That was hours ago. At least we can have a look and see if we can find anything. Come on!'

'Okay, Hannibal, you win. We'll start our explorations by seeking out the kitchen.' So saying, Quentin set off, the others trailing after him.

It didn't take them long; they could smell something cooking and they just followed their noses. At the far end of the entrance room there was a door leading into a corridor. There were two closed doors to their left on the sea side, and one open door on their right. The deliciously promising smell of cooking tickled both their noses and their appetites and led them through the open door.

They found themselves in a big kitchen. 'Good heavens!' said Amaryllis. 'There's something in the oven that smells just like the fish casserole that I prepared at home!' She crossed to the big range cooker on the far side of the kitchen. 'This stove is wood-fired, exactly like the cooker we had on the farm when I was a child!' She opened the oven door. 'Goodness gracious – this *is* my casserole! Those men must have taken it from our house when the neighbours thought they were the police!'

Ambrose laughed. 'Well, I must say you have to hand it to these people. There really doesn't seem to be much that they can't do. Housebreaking is easy for them, it would appear. This casserole must have travelled with us and been put in the oven while we were sitting at the airstrip. Come on, then. What are we waiting for? Let's eat this wonderfully promising casserole. I must say, it smells great!'

They found plenty of cutlery and plates in the drawers. The cupboards were well supplied with food in jars and tins and paper bags, enough food to keep them going for quite a long time. Soon they were sitting round the large table eating the fish casserole that they had thought was so far away in Sprinton Avenue.

When every scrap of the casserole had been eaten, Amaryllis commanded them to do the washing up before exploring. It was then that they realised that all the water in the taps was seawater – and that the water in the hot taps really was hot!

'There must be solar panels,' said Ambrose. 'All very ingenious. I do hope that there is drinking water, too!' There was; they discovered a plentiful supply of drinking water in big glass containers in a corner of the kitchen.

As they explored, the house felt more and more like home. There were two bedrooms and a bathroom on the kitchen side of the house, and two bedrooms and a bathroom on the other side of the great entrance room. In each bathroom there was hot and cold water and a lavatory. It appeared that the rooms had already been chosen for them, for in each one they found their own clothes and belongings from Sprinton Avenue. Not everything, of course – that would have required a pantechnicon – but a goodly selection, none the less.

There was a room for Millicent and Ambrose, a room for Amaryllis and Quentin, a room for Gertrude and Tallulah, and a room for Hannibal. Clothes were already hanging in wardrobes and folded in drawers, and pyjamas and nightwear were neatly laid out on the pillows.

'Goodness me!' said Amaryllis. 'This must be what it's like to stay in Windsor Castle with the Royals! I had a friend who did that once. She was exceedingly embarrassed to see her rather tatty nightie carefully and artistically laid out on the bed!'

'But I'll bet that Windsor Castle doesn't have sea water

in its taps,' said Gertrude.

'Nor get its drinking water from springs and streams,' added Hannibal. 'This place is far more interesting than a palace.'

Each bedroom had a large window, and from each window there was at least a glimpse of the sea. Outside, the moon was casting a shining pathway across the water and the Quintuckles could hear the steady rhythm of the waves rolling in.

Gertrude yawned. 'My bed looks very comfortable,' she said. 'And I'm ready to crawl into it.'

'Wait a minute,' said Tallulah. 'There are two other rooms we've not been into. Let's look inside them before we go to bed.'

Tallulah was quite right. There were two doors on the opposite side of the big entrance room from the kitchen. They opened one of them. The room was all in darkness. 'Find a light switch, someone!' she demanded.

They all started feeling around for a switch. Suddenly Gertrude yelled, 'Found it!' and the room was filled with light.

In the centre was a table with four chairs around it. There were bookshelves from floor to ceiling on all the walls and the shelves were full of schoolbooks covering a great range of subjects – literature and grammar, history, geography, sciences, maths, languages and a whole lot of books of general interest.

'Goodness me!' said Ambrose. 'It's a schoolroom! And

an exceedingly well-equipped one at that! Excellent. It looks as though you lot are expected to continue with your studies! I wonder if a teacher will be provided, or whether it is going to be down to us to educate you! I must say, this Sir Wally seems to have thought of everything! Shall we go and see what surprise awaits us through that other door?'

They filed out. Ambrose closed the door behind them as Quentin opened the other one. Here was an even greater surprise. Every single one of them stood stock still and gazed in amazement. For a long moment there was complete silence. They were completely dumbstruck. And then they all started to speak at once.

'My clarinet!'

'My violin!'

'My double bass!'

'My dulcimer *and* my trombone!'

'My oboe!'

'My saxophone!'

'My flute!'

'My drums!'

'My cello!'

'My xylophone!'

'And a grand piano!'

'Oh, thank goodness!'

'And my piano-tuning kit!'

They looked around the huge space. At one end of the room was a large platform upon which stood a grand piano. All their musical instruments were grouped around the piano. Along one wall were stacks of chairs.

'Goodness,' said Quentin. 'I do believe it's a concert hall.'

'I believe you're right,' said Amaryllis. 'Look, there's a door at the far end. An entrance for the audience, no doubt! Let's see if Paul has been at this piano too.' She went up to the platform and struck a chord. 'Hmm,' she said. 'Obviously not! I'll get to work on it tomorrow.'

'Now I know that I'm dreaming,' said Ambrose. 'This room is almost as big as the Assembly Rooms in Windleford! I really don't think that I can cope with any more surprises at the moment so I'm off to bed. That's the proper location for dreaming. Good night, everyone. I fully expect to wake up in my bedroom in Sprinton Avenue, and then I am going to bore you all with an account of this dream. Good night.' And off he went.

There was a murmur of agreement. Without saying another word, they all turned and followed him. They went to their designated rooms and, in the twinkling of an eye, they were all in bed and sound asleep.

Chapter 6

With windows wide open and the sound of the rolling waves of the sea as a lullaby, every one of the Quintuckles slept soundly for several hours.

Tallulah was the first awake, roused by a loud screeching noise. Opening her eyes she saw, perched on the windowsill, a parrot, a large parrot of dazzling colours, red and green with a shining purple head, gazing straight at her and squawking loudly. It was hardly a very musical sound, but the parrot was certainly an extremely effective alarm clock. Tallulah rolled out of bed as the parrot flew off with a final squawk.

'Golly, what a racket!' muttered Gertrude, and she pulled the duvet up over her head.

Tallulah was now standing by the window, open-mouthed in amazement. 'Quick, Gertie!' she yelled. 'Come and look!'

'Go back to sleep, Tally,' said Gertrude. 'It's much too early for school.'

'No school today, Gertie! Don't you remember where we are?'

Gertrude was suddenly wide awake as all the confusion of the last day and night flooded back into her mind. She threw off the duvet and joined Tallulah at the window. 'Wow!' she said. 'Oh, wow! Maybe being kidnapped isn't so bad after all!'

The two girls stood at the open window and gazed silently at the view spread out before them. The sun was shining on a huge expanse of white sand and blue sea, and there were tall palm trees growing along the shoreline. It was so perfect a scene that it hardly seemed real; it was like a photograph in a travel magazine.

For a long moment there was total silence as Tallulah and Gertrude just gazed and gazed. Then Gertrude suddenly shouted, 'Look! There's someone over there.'

'I can't see anyone! Where?'

Gertrude pointed to the far right of the bay where there was a jumble of rocks at the foot of the cliff. 'Climbing over those rocks,' she said.

And then they shouted together, 'It's Hannibal!'

With one accord, they scrambled into some clothes and were soon in the big entrance hall. The door by the big window was unlocked – they would later discover that there were actually no locked doors on this island – and in a moment the two girls were out of the house, standing in warm sunshine and gazing out to sea. Far out on the huge expanse of water they could see one small rowing boat. There were two people in it.

'They're fishing,' said Gertrude. 'I wonder what they'll catch. Different fish from those we have at home, I expect.'

'Much more exotic, I guess!'

A path led from the back door to the top of the cliff and then descended in a steep rocky zigzag. It was edged by thick thorny bushes before it emerged onto the bare cliff. Gertrude and Tallulah were in such a hurry to reach the beach that they lost their footing several times and slithered and slid down the rough path, but they managed to arrive on the sands below without serious injury, just a few scratches and bruises.

The two girls could now see the whole stretch of beach, which was entirely empty except for a small landing stage running out to sea. A small rowing boat bobbed there. On the beach near the landing stage, facing out to sea, was a noticeboard. The girls ran across the beach towards it. On the board was painted in bold red letters: PRIVATE ISLAND. STRICTLY NO LANDING.

'I wonder if the boat is for us,' mused Tallulah.

'It's on our beach,' said Gertrude. 'So perhaps it is.'

Fortunately, there were no oars in the boat so there was no possibility of trying it out. That was a great blessing as none of the children had any experience whatsoever with boats!

'Maybe there are some oars somewhere up at the house,' said Gertrude. 'We must look. Oh, how I'd love to row out to sea. This boat is obviously meant for us. Look – it's called *The Music Box*! How appropriate! Let's find Hannibal.'

Running along the beach, they headed towards the rocks over which they had seen Hannibal clambering. There was, however, no sign of him. They shouted his name but there was no response.

'Where on earth has he disappeared to?' asked Tallulah.

The two girls kept shouting until at last there was an answering call. Hannibal came into view, scrambling back over the rocks. 'I thought you were never coming,' he said.

'Why didn't you wake us up?' Gertrude asked.

'I couldn't wait to get outside – but I was coming back to fetch you. You absolutely must come and see this amazing rock pool. Come on!'

Hannibal turned and disappeared again behind a rock. Tallulah and Gertrude scrambled after him. Soon they were gazing into a pool of the clearest water they had ever seen. In an instant their shoes were off and they were sitting on its edge, dangling their feet in the water. Brightly coloured small fish swam around their toes. They could see sea anemones, too, so much more colourful than any they had seen on beaches in England.

'I absolutely have to paddle,' Tallulah announced.

'No, better not,' said Gertrude.

'Why not?'

'Remember when you stepped on that sea urchin in Cornwall?'

'Ooh yes, I most certainly do! That really hurt!'

'I'll bet there are loads of sea urchins here,' Hannibal said, 'and they're probably much bigger and spinier than the ones at home. We might need to wear beach shoes when we go into the water. We'll ask – better safe than sorry. Anyway, I think we ought to go back to the house. Mum and Dad will be wondering where we are.'

Just as he spoke, they heard a bell ringing from the house. The sound certainly did carry a long way! As they clambered back over the rocks, they heard the bell again and then Quentin and Amaryllis calling them.

'Coming!' they shouted in reply as they raced back across the sands.

Their parents had descended the zigzag path and were coming towards them. 'We guessed we'd find you down here!' Quentin said.

'There are the most wonderful rock pools over there, full of brightly coloured fish like the ones you see in tropical fish tanks in the wildlife park at home. Come and see!' said Hannibal.

"Yes, come and see!" chorused the girls.

'Later,' said Quentin. 'We have a lot to do first. There are lots of questions to ask, questions that must be answered. I have a few things to sort out with this Sir

Wally, whoever he might be!'

'And some of us have been busy getting breakfast whilst you three have been playing around on the beach,' added Amaryllis.

The three children needed no further encouragement; the word 'breakfast' galvanised them into action. They set off along the beach at a trot. By the time they had reached the top of the cliff path, which was exceedingly rough and steep, they were gasping for breath. They flopped down on the grass and waited for Quentin and Amaryllis to appear, then they all trooped back into the house.

Ambrose and Millicent were in the kitchen, sitting at the table with large cups of coffee in front of them.

'Jolly good coffee,' said Ambrose. 'Do you think they grow their own? Good climate for it, perhaps.'

'Who knows?' said Quentin. 'Anything seems to be possible here.'

'Do you think they grow mangoes?' asked Tallulah hopefully.

'Or pineapples?' Hannibal asked.

'Maybe,' said Amaryllis. "This seems to be a land of infinite possibility!"

'After breakfast we must finish exploring the house,' said Hannibal. 'We haven't had a chance to look inside all those sheds yet.'

'Plenty of time for that later,' said Amaryllis.

'Look, I found this note dropped through the door.'

Millicent took a scrap of paper from her pocket and handed it to Quentin.

'*We will pick you up at 10am to take you to Sir Wally,*' he read out loud. 'Aha! That is a meeting that promises to be very interesting. It promises to be very, very interesting indeed! So, hurry up and eat, everyone, and then we must get ready to go. You can save all your questions for Sir Wally. I've had a snoop around and there's a plentiful supply of writing paper and pens and pencils on the desk in the schoolroom. Let's each make a list of questions we want answered so that we can be sure not to miss anything out. This Sir Wally certainly has a lot of explaining to do!'

'Our lists could be very long,' said Ambrose. 'And our questions could take a long time to answer! What *I* want most to know is exactly whereabouts on this earth *are* we?'

They finished breakfast, but before they had time to even start on their lists they heard the front door opening and then Luke's voice. 'Hi there. Luke here. Are you ready?'

Out they went. Outside was a smaller cart than the one that had brought them to their cabin last night. It had only one horse, quite a big horse, though not as huge as yesterday's Percherons.

Luke was in charge today. He helped each of them up into the cart and then took up the reins.

'What a lovely horse,' said Gertrude. 'What is its name?'

'His name is Jason, and he's a good lad,' said Luke. He clicked his tongue, said, 'Gee up, Jason!' and they were off.

There was silence as they trundled along the track. They were each trying to formulate the one question that they would most like answered and, to be honest, they were all feeling more than a little nervous about meeting Sir Walter. Who exactly was he? It was on his orders that the Quintuckles had been kidnapped and carried to the other side of the world, but what on earth for? What was going on? And what did he intend to do with them now that they were here?

The track ran along the seashore. The sun was shining, the sky was the bluest blue imaginable, and wildflowers were blossoming in profusion. If we were here on holiday, Amaryllis was thinking, we would undoubtedly think this the most beautiful place on earth.

But they were not on holiday; far from it. They had been kidnapped, they had been taken away from their home by force, an experience that had been exceedingly frightening. The children should be in school now and Quentin should be in his office. Amaryllis herself should be pedalling towards someone's out-of-tune piano.

Her mind was in a confusing whirl, but she said nothing as they bumped along. She looked across at Quentin. He was actually smiling as he looked around. Kidnapped or not, he appeared to be really enjoying himself! As indeed he was. At that moment Quentin was thinking that this was far better than sitting in an office all day!

As for Gertrude, Tallulah and Hannibal, they were joggling up and down and grinning. And Ambrose and Millicent were sitting hand in hand, looking around with broad smiles on their faces. Not so very long ago they had all been so anxious and so frightened, but now not one of her family seemed to be in the least bit worried. Amaryllis felt that she was having to do the worrying for all of them.

Hannibal saw the frown on her face. 'Don't worry, Mum. This is an adventure. Whether it will turn out for good or bad we don't know – we'll just have to wait and see. But meanwhile, let's just go along with it.'

'Good advice, Hann!' said Quentin. 'It may all be strange, and we have no idea how things will turn out but, as you say, let's just go along with it! Not that we have a great deal of choice in the matter!'

The horse clopped steadily along the rough track, which wound through cultivated fields to their left and the rocky seashore to their right. Every now and then they passed a group of wooden cabins of varying sizes. In the garden of one of them a young woman was hanging out her washing. She smiled and waved. Otherwise they saw no one.

The steady clip-clop of the horse and the occasional 'Giddy-up' were quite soothing. Millicent, who had not slept very well, would have drifted into sleep if she hadn't been shaken every now and then by violent jolts as the cart hit one of the frequent rough patches on the track.

Rounding a bend, they saw a big wooden cabin in front of them. It was very similar to the Quintuckles' cabin – the place they must now think of as their home. Sprinton Avenue seemed far far away. This cabin was in a wonderful position, perched high up on the cliffs. Beyond it stretched a great expanse of unbelievably blue sea.

There was a cry of 'Whoa!' and the horse stopped. They had arrived at their destination. This must be Sir Walter's home.

The Quintuckles braced themselves. What next, they wondered. Whatever next?

Chapter 7

The Quintuckles clambered down from the cart in silence. Each of them had an image of Sir Walter in their head. They were all imagining a sort of human monster. Ambrose was expecting to meet a terrifyingly austere elderly man. Millicent thought that Sir Walter would be stout and bossy. The image in Quentin's head was that of a retired army officer, harsh and stiff. Amaryllis was imagining a rather pompous, haughty, middle-aged man. The three youngest Quintuckles had discussed Sir Walter and were convinced that he would be like a strict headmaster: very severe, alarmingly stern and distant.

The door of the house opened and a tall man came out to meet them. Surely this couldn't be Sir Walter! He was startlingly young – mid to late twenties perhaps, tall, fair haired, tanned, dressed in jeans and a checked open-necked shirt. He had a big welcoming smile and he held out both hands to them.

'Hello! It is quite wonderful to see you here. I'm Wally or, as many people call me, Sir Wally. When people want to be official they call me Sir Walter, but I'm perfectly happy to be called Sir Wally or just Wally. It is indeed true that I am a knight of the realm but on this island that counts for nothing – though I admit that it does sometimes come in useful when dealing with the world outside.

'I am absolutely delighted to meet you all at last. I've heard so much about you. Shall we go inside and chat? Just take the horse round to the stable, Luke, and then come and join us.'

He beckoned to them to follow and turned towards the cabin. Exchanging glances and raised eyebrows, the Quintuckles, followed him. He was certainly not in the least like any of them had imagined!

This cabin was built on much the same pattern as the one allotted to the Quintuckles. There was the same large entrance room, with its comfortable armchairs and large window looking out to sea.

Gertrude, Hannibal and Tallulah ran across the room to the window. The cliffs were even higher here. They could see the beginning of the path down to the shore and, far below, the rise and fall of the waves. From this angle they couldn't see the beach, but the window was open and they could hear the murmur of the waves breaking on the shore.

'I must say this is very pleasant,' said Ambrose, looking around. 'This cabin is very like the one in which we are installed! And on our way, we passed other log cabins of various shapes and sizes. I imagine you have some local carpenters who are skilled in constructing them. They remind me of family photographs of two of my great-great- uncles who emigrated to Canada many, many years ago. I once visited relatives in British Columbia and was delighted to find that some of the original cabins are still inhabited. Do your builders come from the nearest town? What is it called? Is it nearby?'

Sir Wally laughed. 'Everyone here lives nearby,' he said. 'We are on an island and we do not have any towns – we are just a small community on a small island. And yes, you are quite right about the cabins. All our living spaces are made of wood, a material of which we have an abundance, but the cabins vary a great deal in size. For instance, this house is built on the same plan as yours except that your house has four smallish bedrooms while this house has three big bedrooms. And instead of a concert hall we have the administrative offices.

'I live alone here but right next door is a smaller cabin where Peter and Marina live. Peter runs the office and Marina cooks and cleans. They are absolute treasures, both of them. You'll meet them in a moment. Marina is bringing coffee for us and I've asked Peter to come and join us so that he also can get to know you.

'All our cabins are built on a simple one-storey plan. We have acres and acres of ground so there's no problem with space. We have a plentiful supply of wood and a few skilled builders, plus a lot of willing helpers, so we're getting very good at constructing our homes. One-storey buildings are really fairly simple to build.

'Ah, here is Luke. He is my right-hand man – without him, I would be lost! Now sit down, all of you. Marina will be here soon with coffee. No doubt you have lots of questions. Newcomers always do. I will do my very best to answer them to your satisfaction. By the way, you don't need to introduce yourselves. I know exactly who you all are! And I already know quite a lot about you.'

Sir Wally flung himself into an armchair and looked at the Quintuckles with raised eyebrows.

The Quintuckles all turned to Quentin, who had risen to his feet. 'Well,' he said, 'you may know a great deal about us, but we know nothing whatsoever about you. And we do have a great many questions to ask. The first one is glaringly obvious. We realise that we are on the other side of the world from home, but why exactly are we here – and what right have you to kidnap us?

'You have taken us away from our life in England and brought us to a place which, beautiful as it undoubtedly is, is not where we asked to be. Our questions are legion, and you most certainly have some explaining to do. Perhaps you would start by answering that simple question: why are we here?'

'There is a simple answer to your simple question,' said Sir Wally with a smile. 'You are here to make music, to be our musicians. I firmly believe that music is good for both body and soul and, apart from the Sunday gatherings, there is no music on the island. Oh, sometimes someone hums or sings, but we need music! Everyone needs music!'

'But why us?' demanded Hannibal. 'England is full of musicians, most of them probably much more accomplished than we are!'

Wally laughed. 'Partly because you are a family. I want families on my island that will put down roots. Here you will be able to live happily and peacefully in a self-sustaining community. In addition, I chose your family because you seem to enjoy playing a wide variety of music – and you will most certainly make people happy.

'I heard about you from a friend and asked my men to seek you out, as well as looking at other musicians. As soon as they heard one of your Saturday sessions in the square, they realised that you would be perfect for the island and that they need look no further! I can assure you that you will have very good audiences at your concerts.

'We have no radios and no mobile phones – though I do have satellite communication for emergencies and am able to keep in touch with what's going on in the world. Incidentally, that satellite contact is not available generally on the island – it is strictly controlled. And I am pleased to report that so far – and we've been here for several years now – no one has expressed a wish to leave once they've been here a few weeks, although there have occasionally been difficulties at the very beginning of someone's residency. Are there any more questions?'

'Why kidnap us in such a violent and frightening way?' demanded Tallulah. 'I nearly died of fright. Why didn't you just explain and invite us politely to your island?'

'I'm sorry that you were frightened,' said Wally apologetically. 'I didn't intend that you should be kidnapped in quite that way. I asked my men to get you here somehow and perhaps their ways do seem a little brutal!'

'More than a little, I can assure you,' said Ambrose. 'The children were terrified! In fact, we were all extremely scared. Why did you frighten us with the men wearing those horrid masks?'

Sir Wally frowned. 'I know that the men sometimes wear masks but it's not to frighten you, it is to protect themselves. They don't want to be recognised – there are various reasons for that which we won't go into.

'In answer to your question about why we sort of kidnapped you, we have tried inviting people politely but usually it doesn't work. Most of those who were simply invited turned us down. Some of them told us we were mad; more often people said that it was a nice idea, but they didn't believe that it would work. Fortunately, we didn't reveal our location to any of them, so few people in the outside world know anything about us. And those who do are people we trust, people who will not broadcast our whereabouts.

'I assure you that there is no need for you to worry. There is nothing illegal or improper about us being here. This is my private island, which I inherited as a totally uninhabited wilderness. Incidentally, I wonder what you would have said if my men had just asked you politely if you would like to join us here.'

'We would undoubtedly have turned you down,' said Quentin. 'We have the children's education to think about – and their music lessons. What about my work? What about Amaryllis's piano-tuning job? We have relatives and friends with whom we most certainly do not wish to lose contact. We have responsibilities. We have our life in Windleford. I sincerely hope that you won't keep us here for too long. This is all very beautiful, and I admit that you have looked after us well – apart from the rather brutal kidnapping. This is obviously an intriguing experiment for you but for us it is more than a little disturbing! And being kidnapped was extremely alarming!'

'I do apologise for that,' said Wally. 'Perhaps my men were a little rougher than I realised. But I needed you here and I couldn't run the risk of your turning us down. That could have had serious repercussions. I don't want news of my island to get into the papers. We certainly don't want to be overrun with news reporters and we don't want any publicity. We just want to establish a community that can live independently without damaging the environment.

'It seems to me that the world is getting more and more polluted, both atmospherically and commercially. Mostly we bring in people we know who are sympathetic to our aims and like our way of life. Without exception, all those who have been kidnapped – and there are very few – have all been grateful once the initial shock has worn off. I hope that will be your experience, too. Any more questions?'

'I can see that your intentions are good. You are obviously trying to set up a sort of paradise, your own Utopia,' said Amaryllis. 'But how exactly does it work? For instance, how do we buy food? We have very little money with us, only what the crowd gave us when we played in the square this week. And what currency do you use here?'

'As to food,' said Sir Wally, 'we supply ourselves. The soil is very fertile and we grow our own fruit and vegetables. We also grow and mill corn for flour. There are plenty of fish in the sea and we have animals on the farm – cows and goats for milk and cheese, and chickens for eggs. We eat very little meat.

'Anything that we cannot provide for ourselves is shipped in and distributed as it is needed. We have our own cargo boat that travels to and from Australia. I pay for anything that we ship in and I'm open to requests –

within reason. Don't worry, you won't starve!

'As to currency, we have none. We don't use money on the island because we don't need it. I pay for anything we need to buy from elsewhere. Everyone here has something to offer to others. We choose our residents extremely carefully and do everything by exchange and barter. You, for instance will provide us with music. It's always such a treat when Paul is here to play for us but that is not often. We are looking forward to lots of music now that you're here! There will be no fee for your concerts or for any lessons you give, but you will be richly repaid with food and firewood and whatever else you need.

'As I said, we have the cargo ship. You can order clothes or material for clothing – we have a tailor and a dressmaker amongst our residents – and anything you might need for your home. I will foot the bill in return for the pleasure you will give me with your music.

'We very much hope that you will enjoy being part of our little community. We now have two young farmers and their wives, and four men who are farm workers. Then there are two fishermen, two carpenters, two handymen and a shoemaker. When you need a new pair of shoes, our shoemaker will make them for you – you can even design them yourself! We have a doctor, his wife – who is our nurse – and their son. And we have a dentist, and his wife who is his dental nurse. They are expecting a baby, due very soon! We are all excited at the thought of our first baby on the island. Fortunately, our doctor's wife is a trained midwife and is looking after the mother-to-be. Then there are four general handymen who are also experienced loggers. Big Bob is their chief.

'You know Luke, of course. He is my right-hand man and is tremendously practical. He can turn his hand to pretty well anything. Then there's Robin and the four men who help him with the horses and are also my pilot and aircraft crew. My wi-fi expert is Peter, and his wife is Marina. Between the two of them, they keep me and my house in order. You will soon get to know them all.

'I won't hide from you that some of the islanders are ex-prisoners. I had a great deal to do with the prison service, first in England and then in Australia. Each man was carefully chosen and vetted, and I trust them all.

'One of my ex-prisoners is an excellent artist. Martin spends his working day on the farm, but he paints in his spare time. You will see many examples of his work – he paints what he sees, so in a way his paintings are a history of our little community and our island. He has been here from the beginning. He and I, along with Peter and Marina, were the first residents.

'We also have a retired clergyman and his wife. He runs the Sunday service for us, and he and his wife are good friends to everyone. I'm sure you will enjoy talking to them. The Sunday meeting place has been the big room at the airstrip, but we hope that in future we could meet in your concert room. It would be much larger, and pleasanter too. But only if we have your permission of course.'

'Yes, we would like that,' said Quentin. 'That would be a pleasure. We are the musicians for our church at home – that is we *were*! They will be wondering where we have got to!'

'If you plan to hold your gatherings in the concert room and will have no further use for the piano at the airstrip, then how about moving it to our cabin?' suggested Amaryllis. 'Paul is an excellent pianist. You say that he is coming soon, and two pianos would be useful for both performing and teaching! All of us play the piano – Tallulah, in particular, is a very promising pianist. We could make excellent use of two pianos in the concert room!'

'Indeed yes!' said Wally. 'An excellent idea! I will see to that right away. We are all expected to share our gifts with others. We are a small and very happy community. Now, with all of you here, we have a whole band of musicians, which is wonderful! We hope very much that you will bring a new dimension into our lives.

'So you see, our way of living is not as complicated as you might imagine, though it does require a great deal of organisation. That is mainly my job. You will soon see how it all works. Now, are there any more questions?'

'How long are you planning to keep us here?' asked Quentin.

'I'm hoping that you will enjoy our community. This

is your home now.'

'Oh no,' said Quentin. 'Our home is in England. It is vital that we return there as soon as possible. Surely you can understand that!'

But Wally just smiled and shook his head.

'The children need their education,' said Amaryllis. 'And they need their music teachers. Gertrude has just started lessons with a renowned cellist, which is a great honour. She was specially selected. It is vital that she continues her lessons if she is to become the concert performer that is her hope.'

Sir Wally smiled. 'Maybe she will have a happier life here than life with all the stress of the concert platform,' he said. 'I have heard that can be tough! Now, are there any more questions?'

Before Quentin or Amaryllis could ask anything else, the door opened and in came a young woman with a tray of coffee and biscuits. She was closely followed by a young man. They were very friendly looking. Sir Wally introduced them.

'Marina and her husband, Peter,' he said.

'Are you ready for coffee?' enquired Marina.

'We certainly are,' said Sir Wally. 'And I'm glad that you have done as I asked and brought cups for yourself and Peter. Do join us and meet our musicians!'

'We are so pleased to see you,' said Peter. 'Marina and I both love music and we're much looking forward to your concerts.'

'I am dealing with all their questions,' said Sir Wally with a smile. 'If they have more, perhaps you two can help me to answer them.'

'We do have lots more questions but maybe we have enough to think about for now,' said Amaryllis. 'I'm sure that we shall be bombarding you for some time but I'm not sure that my brain can cope with anything more just at the moment. Those biscuits look delicious!'

Marina handed round coffee for the grown-ups and lemonade for the children, while Peter offered the biscuits.

'I think that you will find us quite civilised!' said Sir Wally. 'I believe we are establishing a better way to live, encouraging respect for the planet. We're not exactly a secret, but we may well be regarded as somewhat secretive! People know that we are here, but we keep ourselves to ourselves. There may well be other similarly reclusive islands – as you are no doubt aware, there are many, many islands here in the South Pacific.'

The Quintuckles sipped their drinks in silence, trying to absorb all that they had heard. Then Millicent spoke up. 'I do have another question,' she said. 'Who makes all the decisions on this island of yours? Do you have some sort of parliament or council?'

'I own the island,' said Sir Wally, 'so I make the decisions.'

'Hmm,' said Millicent. 'That's hardly democratic is it?' She was very outspoken; Millicent was a member of various committees in Windleford and quite used to addressing meetings.

'That's just the way it is, I'm afraid,' said Sir Wally. 'I run the community!'

'Don't take too much notice of Millicent,' said Ambrose with a broad smile. 'She is on all sorts of committees. She loves organising things.'

There was silence for a moment. Sir Wally was looking rather thoughtful. 'Maybe you have raised an important point there, Millicent,' he said. 'Maybe a council, a sort of parliament, would be a good idea. That would be more democratic. Yes, I can see that. I should hate to be thought of as Oliver Cromwell! Thank you for your words of wisdom. I will certainly consider your suggestion. And perhaps, as you have experience, you will help me to sort something out. How would you like that?'

'I accept with pleasure,' said Millicent. 'As Ambrose says, I do love organising things!'

'Right,' said Sir Wally. 'Consider yourself booked!'

Millicent smiled. 'Right,' she said.

'You are taking on a strong woman there,' said Quentin. 'My mother can be quite formidable! Thank you for talking to us. It's a lot to take in and I think we need to think about it and come back to you another day. How do we contact you if there are no telephones? How do we find you?'

'No problems there. I'm around and about all the time and you can always leave a note for me here. But perhaps some of you have more questions now. Fire away!'

'Where do your horses come from?' asked Gertrude.

'The horses are from Australia. They are very hardy and are transported here on the cargo boat. We have a dock for the boat on the eastern side of the island. There is a large cabin there where Big Bob lives, and accommodation for the crew whenever they are here for a few days. Big Bob organises all that. Most of the crew have homes and families back in Australia.

'As I said, at the moment our horses come from Australia but now we plan to breed our own. In fact, the first foals will be born very soon. If any of you are fond of horses, perhaps you would like to help out in the stables?'

'I'd love to,' said Gertrude.

'You will be very welcome,' said Luke. 'I'll go and get Jason now. We will be ready in a moment.'

'Right. Off you go,' said Sir Wally. 'And that reminds me. When you get back to your house, you will find your own transport waiting for you.'

'Our transport?' queried Ambrose.

'Yes, you need to be able to get around the island. I've done my homework, so I knew that at least one of you is good with horses. This is not a big island and you can walk or cycle to any part of it, though cycling is more than a little bumpy on our tracks. We didn't bring your bikes from Windleford because they would be no good on our rough tracks. But I have ordered new mountain bikes for all of you. They will arrive when the cargo boat gets in from Australia in a few days' time.

'By the way, I hear that you, Quentin, are rather clever on that monocycle of yours! I asked my men to bring it along and I'm looking forward to a demonstration! Now, I'm sure that you want to spend a little time exploring the island and getting your bearings. We won't expect too much of you for the next few days. Are there any more questions?'

'There is something that I'm curious about,' said Quentin. 'If you have a cargo boat going to and from Australia, how can you possibly keep your island so private? On the whole, sailors are much travelled and like to talk of their seafaring adventures. Surely they gossip about the island to other sailors that they meet on their travels?'

Wally frowned. 'The island is not exactly a secret!' he said. 'People know of it – indeed it has a name, Hilahila. But people know that it is private and they respect that. They don't attempt to land here.

'There are more than ten thousand islands in this ocean; indeed, the word Polynesia means "many islands". This is by no means the only private island in these waters, though a large proportion of the others have been turned into luxurious holiday resorts for millionaires. Hilahila is very far from that!

'As to our cargo boat, I choose my sailors very carefully. They do not gossip. Most of them have very good reason not to! By the way, you will no doubt have discovered your rowing boat. There are oars in the stables. I don't know how familiar you are with rowing but use the boat only in your bay and stay close to the shore. Don't go out beyond the headland. And there should always be an adult in the boat, at least to begin with.

'Now, I must be getting on if you will excuse me.' The frown disappeared and he smiled. 'We let everyone name their new home. Let me know what you decide. Perhaps you could reflect your position as musicians in your choice. And have you met Geoffrey yet?'

'Geoffrey?' asked Hannibal. 'No. Who is Geoffrey?'

'You'll soon find out! I must get on with the day's work. I shall see you all again very soon. Goodbye.' Sir Wally rose to his feet and briskly left the room.

Chapter 8

'Good with horses!' That phrase was singing in Gertrude's head as they came out of Wally's house. Luke and Jason were waiting for them with the cart. Was it possible that she might soon have a horse to care for? Gertrude was so occupied with her thoughts of horses that she hardly joined in the conversation which the others were having about the visit to Sir Wally.

There was certainly plenty to say. Was Wally mad, or bad, or a mixture of both? Was he a villain, or was he some sort of visionary leader? They all agreed that he was very friendly and that they couldn't help liking him. But at the same time, he expected everyone to do his bidding. He was a conundrum, for sure.

Were they really trapped for ever on this island, away from their home and their friends, away from school and work? What was going on back in Windleford? Was anyone concerned about their disappearance? What would their schools think? Perhaps the police were searching for them. Would it get into the papers? Did anyone care? Perhaps the residents of Sprinton Avenue were only too glad to be rid of them and their multi-coloured door!

And what was all that about the sailors having a good reason not to gossip? Millicent thought she might have the answer to that one. 'I suspect that they are mostly released prisoners, or maybe even wanted by the police,' she said.

'Are you suggesting that the island is peopled with criminals?' asked Amaryllis. 'They don't seem like criminals to me.'

'I'm only saying that *some* of them may have *been* criminals,' Millicent responded.

'Well, I most certainly hope not – though it is undoubtedly true that people who have unfortunate or unhappy lives do often get into trouble for quite minor offences. Sir Wally says he chooses his sailors carefully, and I'm sure he wouldn't have anyone who was violent.'

They stopped talking abruptly as they rounded a bend in the track. They were back at their new home. In front of the house was another cart with a dapple-grey horse in its shafts and a young man in the driving seat.

When Luke pulled up, the Quintuckles clambered out. Gertrude ran straight to the other horse and cart. Could this be for them?

'Hi, Phil,' said Luke. 'Here they all are. I'm handing them over to you! Must go and feed my hens. Cheerio, everyone. This is Phil. See you around.' And with a 'Gee up!' he was off down the track.

Phil was young and very friendly. 'Hi! I'm Phil and I help with the horses. How about you introduce yourselves and I'll try to remember all your names? Though I may get them wrong until I know you all better – there's quite a tribe of you!' They all started speaking at once. 'Steady on!' said Phil. 'One at a time, and let's start with the youngest.'

When the introductions were over, he asked, 'Now, who is going to have the first lesson in handling this horse and cart? I'll take two of you to start with.'

'Well,' said Quentin, 'I guess that had better be me and Gertrude. She is the one who has most acquaintance with horses.'

Phil nodded. 'Have you driven a horse and cart before, Gertrude?'

Gertrude was already clambering onto the cart. 'No, never,' she said. 'But I can't wait to learn. What is the horse called?'

'Her name is Betsy. She's very gentle and a delight to handle. Stanley is great, too – you'll find him in the stable. Horses like company, just like we humans do.'

Quentin climbed up and sat behind Gertrude. Tallulah and Hannibal were eager to get in too, but Phil shook his head.

'I'm sorry but I think we'd better start with just your dad and Gertrude, then they can teach the rest of you,' he said. 'You'll soon get the hang of it. Betsy is very tough – she'll take on almost anything. Why don't the rest of you go and say hello to Stanley? Both horses are good with the cart and you can ride them, too – especially Betsy. Saddles and all the tack you need are in the stable, as well as a bin of carrots. Both these horses love carrots!'

Tallulah and Hannibal needed no second invitation and rushed off to the stable.

'Now, Gertrude, here are the reins,' said Phil. 'Hold them quite loosely. When we're ready to go, give them a shake and at the same time make a little clicking noise with the back of your tongue. I expect you do the same thing when you ride your pony.'

Gertrude nodded. She had thought that she might be a bit nervous to begin with, but she felt quite confident sitting in the cart, reins in hand. 'Come along, Betsy,' she said, giving the reins a little shake. 'Off we go!' Betsy set off at a smart trot along the track, the cart bouncing along behind her. Gertrude laughed with delight. 'Oh, this is amazing!' she said. 'Wonderful!'

'Now, Gertrude,' said Phil, 'the track will divide soon and we'll need to take the right-hand track. You'll need to pull your right-hand rein slightly towards you so that the horse knows.'

As the track divided, Gertrude's slight pull to the right was perfect and soon they were swinging away from the sea and travelling across moorland where sheep were grazing. Ahead of them there was a wood and soon they were amongst the trees.

'You're a natural and no mistake,' said Phil. 'You said that you've never driven a horse and cart before, but have you ever travelled in one?'

'No,' said Gertrude. 'But I'm absolutely loving it!'

'That's obvious!' Quentin laughed. 'And you make it look pretty easy, I must say.'

As the lesson went on, Gertrude found that handling the horse came quite naturally to her. Soon it was Quentin's turn and she reluctantly relinquished the reins. Quentin wasn't quite so quick to pick up the rules as Gertrude, but after a while he got the hang of it.

For ten minutes or so, they rattled along the rough track through the woodland. Then they heard the sound of axe against wood, a cry of 'TIMBER!' and the crunching noise of a falling tree.

Phil shouted, 'Whoa,' and told Quentin to pull on the reins to bring the cart to a standstill.

Out from the trees came three men. 'Hello, there,' Phil said. He turned to the Quintuckles. 'This is Jack and his two sons, Edward and Joel. They are expert woodsmen. There's nothing about trees that they don't know. And here,' he told the three men, 'we have Gertrude and Quentin.'

'Ah! You must be the new musicians. I'm Joel, and this is my little brother, Ed. What sort of stuff do you play?

Not too highbrow, I hope. I'm rather keen on jazz myself.'

'I'm not so little!' Ed said. 'I may be younger than Joel but I'm taller than him! I like a bit of classical, myself, though I like jazz too. And I like to sing a bit.'

'Ed's got a good voice,' said Joel, 'though he can be a bit raucous sometimes.'

Gertrude laughed. 'We play a bit of everything. Let us know your favourites and we'll have a go.'

'We're looking forward to your first concert,' said Jack. 'Come on, boys, back to work. We've lots to do – and no Big Bob today. So, don't forget that I'm in charge!'

'Big Bob's gone on the cargo boat to Australia to get some equipment,' explained Phil to Quentin and Gertrude.

'We're really missing him,' said Joel. 'He's a great boss. He doesn't just tell us what to do – he works as hard as any of us. He often sings his instructions! He's got a great voice, very deep and very strong. You should hear the racket when he and Ed start singing together, especially when the birds join in! But it helps us all to swing an axe or lift a log. Big Bob will probably be away for several weeks. Come and see us when he's back – I'm sure that he'll want to meet the new arrivals!'

'We surely will. Right, Quentin, take us back home,' said Phil. 'When the track divides take the left-hand fork and we'll soon be back at your place. What will you call your cabin, by the way? Have you decided?'

'We'll choose a name this evening,' said Quentin. 'Gee

up, Betsy.'

'Who exactly is Big Bob?' asked Gertrude.

'Big Bob is a giant of a man who heads up the forestry team. He is very tall and very strong but with a somewhat strange character. You can tell that he's Australian by his accent, but I don't know exactly where Sir Wally got him from. Big Bob doesn't talk much. He keeps himself to himself and doesn't have any particular friends, but he's as strong as an ox and very knowledgeable about the trees. I like him. I try to talk to him, though it's very hard to get a word out of him. I've heard that he sings at his work, but I've never heard him. It sounds like we have a treat in store!'

Fifteen minutes later, they made a triumphant return to their new home. All the others, having heard the clip-clop of approaching hooves, came out to greet them.

'Hannibal and I have been having a snoop around,' said Tallulah. 'There are stables – and Stanley is lovely – and sheds, and there's a swing on a branch of that big tree over there. The pram and the monocycle are there but not the tricycle. We've found the oars for the rowing boat and there's a bike there, too.'

'Hands off!' said Phil. 'That's mine! Don't worry, your bikes are on their way. Good strong mountain bikes, one for each of you. The tricycle will be delivered at the same time, and that single-wheel job! We couldn't get everything in the first load. Gertrude has had her first driving lesson and done brilliantly. Hannibal and

Tallulah, now it's your turn. I'm going to give you your first lesson in unhitching the trap and looking after Betsy.'

'Good,' said Quentin. 'That means that I'm free to help sort things in the house. And after lunch…'

'…which will be in half an hour,' said Millicent, turning back into the house. 'I've just put the potatoes on.'

'Great. And after lunch,' continued Quentin, 'I think we'd better gather for a family conference. We have much to discuss! Now, I'm going to do a bit of sorting, starting with the music which is all on the floor in very untidy piles!

'Come on, you three youngsters,' said Phil. 'Let's get Betsy unhitched and take her to the stable to be with Stanley. We'll settle her and Stanley in their new home. They love plenty of attention and are both very sweet tempered, so I'm sure that you will find them great companions.'

Under Phil's instruction, the children and Quentin fed and groomed Betsy and Stanley. Phil was such a good teacher, and Gertrude had such confidence in handling horses, that they soon grasped the practicalities and the horses were quickly settled.

Phil was persuaded to stay and eat lunch with them. After the morning's adventures they were all ravenously hungry. Millicent and Amaryllis had concocted a delicious lunch from the food supplies that they had found stored in the kitchen.

'Great food,' said Phil after they had eaten. 'I really must go now, delightful though it is to be here. By the way, have you met Geoffrey yet?'

'No,' said Hannibal. 'Who is Geoffrey? Sir Wally asked us the same question.'

'Don't worry, you'll meet him soon. Cheerio!'

'Have you far to go?' asked Quentin.

'No distance at all. In fact, I'm your nearest neighbour. I live about a mile along the track. My cabin is called "Cartwheels". You'll find me easily if you want me. I'm here to help any time!' Phil went off to retrieve his bike from the stables where he had left it and pedalled off, bumping along the rough track.

'Well,' said Quentin as they waved Phil off, 'let's hope the tyres on our bikes are as tough as his! But I reckon all the bikes here will be tough or they certainly won't last long. And as his house is called Cartwheels, I guess that he's in charge of all the carts on the island. Maybe he constructs them – or at least makes the wheels!'

That afternoon, the Quintuckles made a start on sorting out the music and their instruments. While they were doing that, they discussed names for the house. Sir Wally had asked that the name should reflect the fact that they were to be the island musicians. After lots of suggestions, agreements and disagreements, they each picked just one name, wrote it down on a scrap of paper, folded it and put it into Gertrude's straw hat.

These were their suggestions:

Ambrose – The Music Shack

Millicent – Drumbeat

Amaryllis – Octaves

Quentin – Strummings

Gertrude – Harmony

Hannibal – Cacophony

Tallulah – Sea Shanty

Gertrude gave the hat a good shake and held it up high. Tallulah, as the youngest, pulled out a slip of paper and unfolded it. It was Ambrose's suggestion, "The Music Shack", and thus their house was named.

Quentin carefully painted The Music Shack above the door and decorated it with a few notes of music. Anyone with a knowledge of musical notation could have discerned that the few notes are the opening notes of the old song, 'Oh I Do Like To Be beside the Seaside'. That made them all laugh. They reckoned that The Music Shack was a good name, and the words of the old music hall song very apt for the Quintuckles and their situation!

Quentin started to sing: 'Oh I do like to be beside the seaside,' and they all joined in:

'Oh I do like to be beside the seaside

I do like to be beside the sea

I do like to stroll along the prom-prom-prom

Where the brass band plays tiddly-om-pom-pom.'

'Speaking of which,' said Hannibal, 'I quite fancy a

stroll down to our "prom" –the beach. Anyone coming with me?'

'Oh yes!' chorused Gertrude and Tallulah.

'Race you down there!' shouted Hannibal as he set off at a run.

They heard Amaryllis calling after them. 'Supper in an hour so don't be too long. Be careful!' But they failed to hear the rest of the sentence: 'And don't go wandering too far. You don't know your way around yet! We don't want you getting lost!'

But, as it turned out, not only were the three children going to wander a long way, they were also going to get lost. They were going to get very lost indeed!

Chapter 9

Hannibal was in the lead with Gertrude and Tallulah following him down the rocky twisting path to the beach. 'Shall we paddle?' he asked.

'No,' said Gertrude. 'Let's explore.'

They ran across the sands towards the rocky headland where they had discovered all the rock pools. They went from pool to pool, peering into the clear water, seeing all sorts of brightly coloured plants and creatures.

One of Gertrude's shoes came off as she scrambled over the rocks and it dropped down into a crevice. To her dismay, it disappeared from view and she had to push her hand down and feel around.

Eventually she located it, but the rocks had her shoe in a vice-like grip and Gertrude had a struggle to pull it out. Eventually she succeeded, sat on the rocks and pushed her foot into it. There was something inside it, something that was moving!

Gertrude yelped, pulled out her foot and peered into her shoe. It was a crab, small and very pretty, bright pink with white spots. She shook the shoe and the little crab dropped out and scuttled away, disappearing quickly into a crack in the rocks.

Pulling on her shoe, Gertrude jumped down from the rocks onto the sand. She looked for Hannibal and Tallulah, but they were nowhere to be seen. She shouted their names; no answer. She shouted again, as loud as she could, 'Hannibal! Tallulah!' This time there was a distant answering shout that seemed to come from the trees along the shore.

'Where are you?' she yelled.

'In the woods,' came the reply.

'Keep shouting!'

'We're not very far in. We'll come and meet you. Shout again when you get past the coconut palms.'

Once Gertrude was beyond the palm trees, which fringed the shoreline, she found herself facing a seemingly endless forest of huge trees, trees that looked as if they each had several trunks all tangled together. Their branches were thick and twisting; Gertrude had never seen trees back home that looked anything like these. There was no discernible path.

'Where are you?' she shouted. She was relieved that, although she couldn't see Hannibal and Tallulah, their answering shouts of 'Over here!' sounded quite near.

'Don't move!' she called. 'But keep shouting!'

It took quite a few shouts and a great deal of scrambling before the three of them were re-united.

'Where have you been? We were on our way back to find you. We thought you were following us,' said Hannibal.

'My shoe got stuck in the rocks. Why didn't you wait for me?'

'Sorry, we didn't know that you were stuck – we just assumed that you were behind us,' Hannibal replied.

'We'd better stick together from now on, at least until we know our way around,' Gertrude said.

'Right. Come on, let's explore. We've been hunting for a path, but we haven't found one yet.' Hannibal was eager to keep going.

They set off through the maze of trees but without any paths they had no idea which direction they were going in. The strange, tangled trees around them all looked much the same and seemed to go on for ever.

'I think we'd better turn around and go back to the beach,' said Tallulah. 'At least then we'll be able to find our way back to the house. We don't want to get lost!'

'Good thinking,' said Hannibal. 'Better safe than sorry. Let's turn around.'

They turned and tried to retrace their steps through the trees but, although they kept stopping to listen for the sound of the sea, they heard only the rustling of the leaves overhead and the sound of their own footsteps. They couldn't hear the surf rolling onto the beach and there was no open sky above them, just trees, trees and more trees!

The children realised that they had no idea of the direction they were walking in. Surely the wood must end somewhere! After about half an hour of wandering, they sat down on the trunk of a fallen tree and tried to work out where they should go.

'I've got my whistle in my pocket,' said Hannibal. 'I'll blow it in case there's anyone around who might come and find us.'

'I doubt if there's anyone around at this time of day,' said Tallulah. 'Everyone will have stopped working and gone home for supper.'

'Well, it's worth a try,' said Hannibal. He always carried a piercing whistle in his pocket, together with his Swiss Army knife. Whenever he was teased about it, he always said it was good to prepare for emergencies.

'I don't think it will do any good,' said Gertrude. 'We must be a long way from the house now – and we don't even know in which direction home is! We seem to have lost the sea completely and there is no sign of any habitation around here.'

Nonetheless, Hannibal stood up and blew his whistle. It was exceedingly powerful and the sound it made was certainly very loud and very piercing. He blew three short blasts followed by three long blasts and then another three short ones. 'SOS,' he said, laughing.

There was a moment's silence and then a cacophony

of squawking and trilling. The whistle seemed to have stirred up every bird in the forest but, although they listened hopefully for a few minutes, there was no other response, no shouts, no whistles.

After a few minutes, even the birds stopped protesting. Hannibal tried the SOS whistle blasts again but still there was no response, except for the re-awakened birds chirruping and squawking in the trees.

The three children set off again, although they had absolutely no idea where they were going. After what seemed like an age, they stopped and looked around. But all they could see in every direction were huge, multi-trunked trees – trees, trees and more trees. They set off again, quickening their steps until they were quite out of breath.

'Listen,' said Tallulah for the umpteenth time. 'Let's listen for the sea again.' But all they could hear was the sound of their own laboured breathing and the chirping and whistling and squawking of the birds.

'I'll try the whistle again,' said Hannibal. He put his hand in his pocket but was shocked to find that the whistle wasn't there. He tried all his pockets and pulled out his Swiss Army knife, but still there was no whistle. 'Oh no! I must have dropped it somewhere,' he said. 'How on earth did that happen? We'll just have to keep moving. If we can manage to walk in a straight line, we must get somewhere eventually!'

'Let's shout,' said Tallulah. 'If we all shout together it

will make quite a racket. Maybe there is someone nearby.'

'I doubt it. Please can we just sit down for a minute and catch our breath?' And Gertrude flopped down onto the ground.

'We could tell which way to go from the direction of the sun,' said Hannibal. 'But the trees are so dense and the sun so low that it's difficult to work out just where it is.'

'And anyway, it's all different on this side of the world,' Tallulah said gloomily, recalling geography lessons about the rising and the setting of the sun in different parts of the globe. 'Let's just rest for a moment, then try again to get back to the beach.'

'I still think it's worth shouting,' protested Hannibal. 'At least we can have a go!'

'Okay. Worth a try,' said Gertrude.

They all took deep breaths then shouted together as loudly as they could. They managed to make a considerable noise, but their 'halloo' quivered in the air for a moment and then faded away into the forest with no answering shout. They had only succeeded in stirring up the birds again.

'Let's have one more try,' said Hannibal. They each took a deep breath and then once more shouted together as loud as they could. But again, their cries faded away with no answering shout.

'We'll keep moving,' said Gertrude. 'But we must try to keep going in a definite direction and not walk round in circles. Surely we'll get somewhere if we walk straight enough. The wood must end eventually.' She was trying to sound calm and sensible but in reality she was starting to feel very frightened. Would they ever get out of this wood? Surely someone would search for them if they didn't return home – but would anyone find them amongst all these trees?

'Look!' said Tallulah suddenly. 'Isn't that the fallen tree we sat on earlier? It looks the same. If it is, we've just walked for what seems like hours in an enormous circle. We're back where we started.'

Hannibal rushed to the tree and scrabbled on the ground. He straightened up, looking triumphant. He had his whistle in his hand. 'It *is* the same,' he said, 'and here is my whistle. All that walking, and we're back where we were! But at least we know that we're not that far from the sea. And, what is more, I have my whistle back.' He blew another SOS, but again the only response was the protesting of the birds.

'That's not working,' said Gertrude. 'Save your breath. Let's sit down for a minute and think what to do next. We have to work out a plan.'

They sat on the log. They were tired, they were dispirited – and they were undoubtedly completely lost. Try as they might, they couldn't think of a plan, and they sat side by side in gloomy silence.

Chapter 10

Back at the newly named The Music Shack, the grown-ups were beginning to get anxious. Surely the children should be back by now. Quentin had just returned from the beach and reported that there was no sign of the children down there. 'They must have gone into the woodland behind the beach,' he suggested.

Amaryllis was fearful. 'If they don't return soon, we'll have to get help – but how do we go about that? We don't know who to ask. We don't know whether anyone lives close by. We have no telephone, no car. We don't even have a map. What can we do? Where do we start? And it will be getting dark soon.'

Quentin tried to console her. 'Don't worry,' he said. 'They're sensible. And after all, they're not babies. Let's be patient. They'll turn up soon, I'm sure.' But truth to tell, he was not sure. He wasn't sure at all!

The Quintuckles had been transported against their will to the other side of the world, to a place which was totally alien to them. They had no idea what dangers might lurk in this unknown place. And it was certainly true, as Amaryllis said, that there was no telephone and no handy car into which Quentin could leap to go for help. And no hospital available should he find any of the children injured! What to do indeed?!

And then Quentin had an idea. Phil! He'd cycle to Phil's cabin. But, of course, he had no bicycle! The tricycle, then? But the tricycle, along with the pram, the trailer and the monocycle, was still at the airfield. Then he had the answer: he must take one of the horses. He was fairly sure that he could remember how to get to Phil's home and Phil knew the island well. He would surely have some idea of where the children might be.

'Don't worry, Amaryllis. I'll find them.' Quentin ran out of the house before she could question him as to how he was intending to do that.

In the stable he decided that it was best to try and harness Betsy. He remembered Phil telling Gertrude that Betsy was particularly amenable to being ridden. He had a bit of trouble finding the right harness but, once he had found it, it was not as difficult to put it on her as he had feared.

Betsy seemed quite happy and stood quietly while Quentin hoisted himself into the saddle. She turned out to be amenable and co-operative, and soon they were heading along the track towards Phil's home. Phil had said that he was their nearest neighbour so it shouldn't be too far.

The sun was low in the sky and Quentin was getting anxious, though he'd not admitted as much to Amaryllis. He was relieved when he spotted the roof of a cabin among the trees on the right-hand side of the track ahead of him. Sure enough, as he rode up to it, he saw the name CARTWHEELS carved into a board above the door. This was definitely Phil's cabin.

He was surprised to find a horse tethered there. He was about to dismount when the door opened and out came Phil, followed by Luke.

'Goodness!' Luke said. 'I didn't expect to see you tonight! You're looking worried. What's the matter?'

Quentin explained the situation and told them how anxious Amaryllis was. 'What should we do?' he asked. 'Have you any ideas?'

'Did they have bathing things with them?' asked Phil.

'No.'

'Then they won't have gone into the sea. That's good. Most of the bathing is safe, but it can be a bit dangerous near those rocks. They'll be somewhere in the woods. Don't worry, we have no savage animals on the island. But the children could easily wander for hours and not find a way out, especially with the light fading. I'm sure we can find them.'

'No, don't you worry, Phil,' said Luke. 'I'll go. I was just leaving, and Darwin is very eager to move on.'

'That makes sense, but let me know if you need me,' Phil said. 'I'm happy to help. Good luck – I'm sure you'll find them soon.'

'It's good to see that you chose to ride Betsy. She's a good horse, as is my Darwin. He's named after one of my heroes,' said Luke as he and Quentin set off down the track.

'Don't worry, children,' murmured Quentin to himself. 'Help is on the way. Luke knows his way around.' How he hoped that he was right. 'Where are we heading?' he asked aloud.

'First of all, we need to see if we can find Geoffrey,' Luke replied.

'Geoffrey?' said Quentin. 'Who on earth is Geoffrey? Sir Wally mentioned a Geoffrey, I think. Then you did – and now you've mentioned him again!'

Luke laughed. 'You'll find out. He and his shadow are the best trackers on the island. He'll be able to find the children, I'm sure. He lives a bit further along the track. Let's hope that he's in – I think that there's a good chance that we'll find him there at this time of day.'

'You mention his shadow,' said Quentin. 'Who is that?'

Luke laughed again. 'Not exactly a "who",' he said. 'You'll soon find out!'

Chapter 11

Gertrude, Hannibal and Tallulah were still sitting on the fallen log trying to decide on their next course of action. The light was fading fast – twilight didn't seem to last very long on this side of the world.

'Let's move on,' said Hannibal. 'We can't sit here any longer.'

'I don't think we should go any further,' said Gertrude. 'It's too dark. We'll just have to stay here all night. I hope there are no dangerous wild animals around.'

'Or snakes,' muttered Hannibal.

Tallulah shuddered at the thought of snakes. 'I think that Hannibal is right. We should move on,' she said. 'If we walk in a straight line, surely we must get somewhere eventually.'

'Perhaps they'll send a search party out for us,' said Gertrude.

'I doubt it.' Tallulah looked glum. 'And even if they do, they'll have no idea in which direction we went. It's our own fault. We should have stayed on the beach.'

'I really think it's best to stay put,' said Gertrude. 'We might get even more lost if we go in the wrong direction.'

'They'll guess that we're in the woods when they see that we're not by the sea,' said Hannibal. 'I think we should keep walking but try to stay in a straight line, then we're bound to come out somewhere. This wood must end eventually. Come on!' He got up and started walking through the trees in a very determined way.

'Come back, Hann!' cried Gertrude. 'We must stick together.' But Hannibal kept walking, and the two girls had no option but to follow him.

'Blow the whistle again, Hann,' said Gertrude.

'No point,' said Hannibal, but all the same he took the whistle out of his pocket. He would give it one more try.

The silence of the woods pressed down on them. There was no bird song, no footsteps, no voices, no sound at all.

The three children huddled together. Hannibal took a deep breath and put the whistle to his lips. Again, the SOS streamed through the trees and again, the birds were disturbed and set up a loud chattering.

The three children were getting tired, but they plodded on. They had lost all sense of direction. 'Let's stop for a few minutes,' said Tallulah, and she sat down on the ground. The other two were only too glad to rest for a moment and plonked themselves down beside her. The clatter of the birds died away, and they sat together in silence. They were exhausted.

Eventually Gertrude spoke. 'Blow again, Hann,' she said. 'It probably won't do any good, but we have to keep trying.'

Hannibal pulled the whistle out of his pocket and raised it to his lips but, before he could blow, there was the crack of a twig, the creak of a branch, the swish of leaves—

The three children sat frozen to the spot. It was getting darker but there was still light enough to see that the trees were stirring. Something was moving in the wood, something was coming towards them, something very much bigger than a bird…

They huddled together, hardly daring to breathe. Whatever it was, it was coming nearer. They could hear branches rustling and the panting of an animal. Yes, an animal was moving towards them. The panting came nearer and nearer, nearer and nearer…

Chapter 12

Luke was trying to reassure Quentin as they rode on. 'I'm sure the children will be fine, though I do understand your anxiety. If I didn't know the island as well as I do, I would be anxious too. Ah! Here's the surgery. Let's hope that Geoffrey is in.'

Luke swung from the saddle, walked to the cabin door and knocked. There was no sound of movement from within. He knocked again. Still no response. He called out, but there was no reply. He went round to the back of the cabin but soon came back. It was obvious that neither Geoffrey nor anyone else was in the cabin with the word 'THE SURGERY' on the sign above the door.

'Is Geoffrey a doctor?' asked Quentin.

'No. He's the doctor's son,' replied Luke.

'Oh! How old is he?'

'Around twelve, I think.'

'And he's a good tracker?'

'None better. Though tracking in the dark is more than a bit tricky, and there's not much light left.'

'Where might we find him?'

'He could be anywhere on the island. It's a pity that neither he nor his parents are here. They may have been called out. Geoffrey's parents are our doctor and our nurse – Doctor Tom and Nurse Joyce are very much loved and needed! We'll just have to do our best without Geoffrey. I'll pop into the house and leave a message.'

'Do you have a key?'

Luke laughed. 'Nobody on the island has a key. We don't need keys.'

'Oh yes, I forgot. Sir Walter told us that. I haven't got used to it yet.'

As Quentin waited for Luke outside the cabin, he got more and more anxious. As the light faded, he became conscious of all sorts of sounds – birdsong, the rustling of leaves, a distant, long drawn-out whistling sound. The island is full of noises, he thought, and imagined an enraged Caliban rampaging through the forest.

Luke was soon swinging himself back into the saddle. 'Don't fret,' he said, looking at Quentin's worried face. 'We'll find them.'

'But I'm hearing all sorts of strange noises, "tongues in trees" as Shakespeare says. Croaking and a loud whistling. What could that be? What about wild animals?'

asked Quentin.

'It's the birds, they can be very noisy! There are no dangerous animals on the island to harm them, but if your children are indeed in the woods – which is very likely – then there is every possibility that they are lost. They may well be walking around in circles. There aren't really any paths except for this main track and a smaller track that goes off it down to the beach. Nevertheless, I'm sure that we'll find them soon.'

'I do hope so,' said Quentin. But in truth he was getting more and more alarmed. He knew that his children were resourceful and sensible, but they had been through a very traumatic experience and now they were in a strange and puzzling place.

Luke's voice broke into his gloomy thoughts. 'Don't worry. The wood is dense but it's not very big. We're just coming to the point where we swing onto the narrower track that goes through it. We'll have to go in single file. The children are most likely to be away from the track or they would have found their way out, but there's no way that we can take the horses in amongst the trees. My guess is that the children started from the beach on the track but then left it to explore the woodland. They probably plunged in without realising how quickly they might get lost.'

It was getting darker now and Quentin was trying not to show how anxious he was. Maybe the children were home by now. There was no way of communicating with

Amaryllis to find out. He must continue searching.

They soon came to the point where the track divided. They took the narrower track off to the left which took them deeper into the wood. Luke rode in front with Quentin following him. They rode in silence, listening for any sign or sound of the children. On every side of the track the tangled trees looked impenetrable. Every now and then they paused to shout 'Halloaaa', but the only response was the chattering and squawking of the birds. There was no welcome answering shout from the children.

Chapter 13

'It's coming this way,' whispered Hannibal. 'It must be an animal of some sort. Don't move. It might be dangerous. It might just pass us by. Shhhh!'

They clung on to each other and kept as still as they could. The rustling in the undergrowth came nearer, then suddenly a dark shape, a black animal of some sort, emerged from the trees. It was too dark for the children to identify it as it came towards them, sniffing the ground.

'What is it?' Tallulah gasped. 'It's coming straight for us.'

Suddenly it was upon them. Gertrude screamed as it leapt at her.

'It's a dog,' said Hannibal. 'And it doesn't seem fierce at all. In fact, it seems very pleased to see us!' The dog was wagging its tail furiously.

'Don't worry,' shouted a voice from somewhere in the trees. 'It's only Reggie. He's very big but he's very friendly.'

The voice was followed by a body appearing from the trees. It was the body of a boy. A small boy. A very small boy indeed. He grinned at them. 'Oh!' he said. 'You must be the new arrivals! I should have guessed! So that was *your* whistle I heard sending out an SOS. I wish you'd kept on blowing it, it would have made finding you much easier. I would have had to wait till daylight tomorrow to be able to actually track you! It was fortunate that you eventually sent a second SOS that sent me in your direction. Once Reggie got your scent, we came straight for you.

'I knew you'd arrived on the island and I was looking forward to meeting you, but I didn't think it would be like this, with you lost in the middle of the woods. I was planning to come and visit you in your cabin tomorrow.'

The Quintuckle children stared at the boy. He looked much too young to be alone in the woods, even with his dog. Eventually Gertrude broke the silence. 'Hello,' she said politely. 'We're most awfully glad to see you. We're the Quintuckles, by the way. I'm Gertrude. I'm the oldest. I'm thirteen.'

'And I'm Tallulah. I'm ten.'

'We're new here, and we've managed to get ourselves lost. So silly! I'm Hannibal. I'm twelve.'

'Well, I'm Geoffrey and I'm twelve too! Welcome to Hilahila. I'm so glad that you're here. You're the new musicians with the very funny surname. I knew that Sir Wally was trying to get you to come.'

They stared at him. So this was the Geoffrey that Sir Wally had mentioned. But he was so small! Twelve? He couldn't possibly be twelve. He looked much younger.

Geoffrey grinned as he looked at their astonished faces. 'I know I look much younger than I am. I was a very premature baby. Dad says I might have a bit of a growing spurt and look more normal later on, but I'll probably just be little all my life. I don't mind. It can be quite useful sometimes.'

There was silence as the Quintuckle children continued to stare at him. Could someone so small really be twelve years old? Tallulah was the first to find her voice. 'We have heard about you – Sir Wally mentioned you. Are there lots of other children here?'

'No, just me. But my mum and dad, who are the doctor and nurse on the island, are busy delivering a baby right now – the first baby on the island. I'm so glad that you've come. It's so exciting that you're here.'

'Hmm.' Gertrude was not so sure. At that moment, she felt certain that she would rather be back in Windleford! 'What happens about school?' she asked. 'Do you have any lessons?'

'Oh, there's no school on the island,' said Geoffrey.

'No school! Yippee!' said Hannibal.

'But I certainly don't escape education! My mum and dad teach me a bit. And you might well say "Yippee!" but it gets very frustrating to be taught by your parents! And although I know quite a bit about the human body and how it works, which I suppose might come in useful, I really don't know much else. Mum and Dad are pretty good on Biology and Physics and not bad on Chemistry, but they are extremely vague about most other things. What about yours?'

The three Quintuckles thought about it and decided that their parents could cover Music, Literature and perhaps a bit of Geography, but not much else.

'So, you don't have any friends,' said Tallulah. 'No one to play with. Poor you!'

'I have Reggie,' said Geoffrey. 'He came from Australia. One of the crew brought him over on the cargo ship. He found him wandering alone when he was only a puppy and thought he would be company for me. Reggie comes everywhere with me and everyone loves him – it's not the same as having a human friend though. But now I have the three of you, which is great. Come on, I think we'd better get moving. I know where your cabin is of course, but it can be awfully tricky to find the way through the woods in the dark. Keep close behind me. Best not to get separated, though Reggie will probably round us up if we do.'

'Are there dangerous animals in these woods?' asked Tallulah.

'There are no dangerous animals anywhere on the island,' said Geoffrey. 'In fact, there are no wild animals at all. There are quite a few pet dogs that have been brought in from Australia. Sir Wally doesn't allow any hunting dogs, or dogs which might be a danger to people or birds. There are plenty of birds, parakeets and pigeons and terns and things. You've no doubt heard them. They make an awful lot of noise when they get going!'

'What about snakes?' Tallulah asked.

'No snakes,' said Geoffrey. 'But lots of bats. Flying foxes, we call them. They have the sweetest faces. They love to roost in these old fig trees.'

'Is that what these trees with the tangled roots are?' asked Gertrude. 'We keep tripping over them. They look frightfully old.'

'This wood is mostly ancient banyan trees and fig trees and they all have very tangled roots! You certainly have to watch where you're going. Come on, we need to move. Let's get to the track first, then it will be an easy walk to the beach. When you get to the sea, you'll know where you are. Follow me.'

'But we thought that the tide was coming in. Will there still be enough beach to walk on?' Hannibal asked.

Geoffrey laughed. 'No problem there,' he said. 'The tide comes in and out regularly, but it makes hardly any difference to the beach as it only comes in a little way. The other strange thing is that it comes in and out at the same time every day. My dad says that's not usual. Let's go! We're not far from the only track that goes through the wood. Follow me – and stay close. We must all stick together. Best to stay in single file – and be careful where you put your feet because the tree roots wander off in all directions! We don't want anyone falling over and breaking a leg! Come on.'

Geoffrey set off with Hannibal close behind him, followed by Tallulah and Gertrude. Reggie rushed about rounding them all up and making sure that no-one was left behind.

'Do you like living here, Geoffrey?' asked Gertrude.

'Most of the time,' replied Geoffrey. 'But I've never lived anywhere else, so I don't know what anywhere else is like – except what I read in books. It's a bit lonely with no other children of my age here. I talk to Reggie a lot, but he is a bit short of words though he does know a few. He understands words like "walk" and "treat". And he knows the word "home", which is very useful if I find myself a bit lost. I put him on the lead and say, "Home, Reggie," and he takes me back to our cabin. He's not failed me yet! And he is most awfully good at wagging his tail! Yes, Reggie is a very good friend, but I was thrilled when I heard that there was a whole family of children coming to live on the island.'

'How long have you been here?' asked Hannibal.

'I was born here.'

'You were *born* here?'

'Yes. Apparently, my mum and dad's journey here was a bit of a disaster. They had to make an emergency landing on the way. Mum was expecting me and, because of the shock, she had me the day after they arrived. I was eight weeks early – that's why I'm so little for my age. Apparently, it was amazing that I survived because there was no equipment here for premature babies. But I'm here! Good job my dad was a doctor!'

'We were kidnapped!' said Tallulah. 'We were just going back home after our Saturday session in the square when…'

'Shhhhh!' said Geoffrey, putting his finger to his lips and turning away from the direction in which they were heading. They all turned round as he whispered, 'Don't move. Listen!'

The children stood in silence, straining their ears. At first they heard nothing, and then there was a faint thudding and a distant call. They sensed a movement in the branches. Something was coming towards them. Something big was moving through the trees…

Tallulah's knees felt very shaky. She thought she might fall – and there was certainly no chance that she could run. 'I thought you said there were no dangerous animals,' she whispered.

'There aren't.' Geoffrey grinned. 'Don't worry, we're nearly at the track. Those are horses. My guess is that someone is looking for you.' He cupped his hands to his mouth and shouted, 'Hello there!' For such a little person, he had a surprisingly loud voice.

'Hello!' came an answering voice. 'Is that you, Geoffrey?'

'Yes! And I've got the new children with me. We're not

far from the track. Could you wait where you are until we get clear of the trees?'

'Right. We'll wait here.'

'That's Luke,' said Geoffrey. 'Come on. We're nearly there.'

A few minutes later, they emerged from the trees onto a rough track. In the middle of the track were two men on horseback – Quentin and Luke.

'I assume that these are your lost children?' said Luke.

'They are indeed,' said Quentin, looking and sounding very relieved.

'I might have known that it would be you, Geoffrey, who got to them first!' said Luke.

'It was quite by accident. I went outside to shut the chickens up and heard this whistle in the woods. As it was blowing an SOS call, I knew it wasn't an animal or bird so I came to see what was going on. Reggie was with me, of course, and between us we found them quite easily. They were lost in the middle of the trees, just like the Babes in the Wood!'

'It's a very good job you found them and got them to the track,' Luke said. 'We couldn't have taken the horses into that tangle of roots and branches. We were just about to continue our search on foot, so you've saved us a lot of trouble. You must take them back to their cabin as fast as you can because they have a very anxious mother waiting for them! We'll take the horses back up the track – they can't manage that path up the cliff face!

111

Don't worry, children, Geoffrey will get you safely back to your cabin. By the way, Quentin, I forgot to ask you if you've decided on a name for your place yet.'

'We're calling it The Music Shack.'

'Good name,' said Geoffrey. 'I like that. Mum and Dad tried to call our cabin "Arcadia", which apparently means Paradise. Once they'd been here for a few weeks and got over the shock of me being born prematurely, they decided that this really was a sort of paradise. Mum painted the sign to put over the door but everyone just called it "The Surgery", so eventually Mum and Dad gave in. Mum made a new sign, and we gave Arcadia to some new arrivals who liked the name.'

'Right then. We'll all meet up at The Music Shack and then, Geoffrey, I'll give you a ride back to The Surgery. You left a note for your parents I hope?' Luke asked.

'Yes, I did. They won't worry.'

'Fine. Off we go then, Quentin. Back up the track.'

Luke and Quentin turned the horses around and set off back along the track, while the children followed Geoffrey towards the beach. Even though it was now dark, the moon was up and almost full and it was an easy walk because there were no tree roots to trip over or to get entangled with. It didn't take them long to get back to the seashore and soon they were over the rocks, along the beach and heading up the zigzag track to the house.

Chapter 14

In The Music Shack, Amaryllis, Ambrose and Millicent were anxiously waiting for news. Amaryllis had been trying to keep busy in order to stop imagining all the dreadful things that she feared might be happening to the children. She had laid out a feast on the kitchen table in the hope that soon they would all be home, laughing about their adventures. Now she was playing the piano, hoping that the music might take her mind off the missing children – but in that she was not succeeding.

She was not alone in being worried. Ambrose and Millicent, although they were trying to reassure Amaryllis, were getting very fearful. The curtains were wide open. Night had fallen, and outside everything appeared ghostly and mysterious in the moonlight. The area was unknown. How on earth were the children going to find their way back home?

When they heard laughter and chattering outside, they rushed to the door and flung it open. Amaryllis was so relieved that she burst into a mixture of laughter and tears. 'Wherever have you been? Dad has gone to look for you. Thank goodness you're back. We have been imagining all sorts of disasters.' Then she spotted Geoffrey, who had been hanging back. 'Hello,' she said. 'And who are you?'

'This is Geoffrey,' said Gertrude. 'He heard Hannibal's whistle and he came into the woods to find us. He's brilliant. He rescued us.'

'Really?' said Amaryllis, looking doubtful.

Geoffrey laughed. 'I expect you think I'm too young to be wandering alone in the woods, but I'm older than I look. I'm twelve. I'm just very short.'

'Twelve! Really?'

'Yes. I know that it's hard to believe when I'm so little.'

'Oh, Geoffrey, I do apologise,' Amaryllis said.

Geoffrey laughed. 'Don't worry. I'm used to it!'

'I don't know how you did it but thank you very much for your rescue effort. I suppose your parents knew that you were going into the woods?'

'I left a note. They've been called out to deliver a baby.'

'Geoffrey's father is a doctor,' said Tallulah. 'And his mother is a nurse,' she added.

'Oh, I see,' said Amaryllis, thinking that this strange island was full of extraordinary surprises. 'Quentin is out looking for you all. I think he was going to try to find Luke. Oh dear! With no telephones, how are we to let him know that you're safe? I do hope that he won't get lost, too.'

'Don't worry, Mum,' said Gertrude. 'Dad's fine. He found Luke and they came together to look for us. We met up with them in the woods. They couldn't come home with us because they had to stick to the track with the horses. The trees are much too thick and tangled for the horses to get through, so they've had to go the long way round. Dad's looking extremely comfortable and happy up on Betsy! He should be here soon. Is there anything to eat? I'm starving!'

'I'm sure that you are *all* hungry! There's plenty of food on the table in the kitchen. Go and help yourselves.'

The children went to the kitchen and soon were sitting round the table, eating and chattering. They were indeed extremely hungry after their woodland adventures.

'You have no idea how happy I was when Mum and Dad told me that you were coming,' said Geoffrey. 'But I was a bit worried that you might not be friendly. Mum said that you were a family of musicians and you might all be very grown-up and serious.'

'Well, as you can see, we're not at all grown up,' said Tallulah.

'But we are of course *very* serious,' said Hannibal, pulling down the corners of his mouth and trying to make his face as stern as possible.

'Don't be silly,' said Gertrude. 'And don't pull that face. The wind may change and then you might stay like that for ever, like the little girl in the fairy story.'

Geoffrey laughed. 'I'm so glad that you are here. It's not much fun being the only child.'

'Did you and your parents get kidnapped and bundled into a van like we did?' asked Tallulah.

'No, not quite,' said Geoffrey. 'My father was a friend of Sir Wally's in England. They were at school together. Apparently, they used to say that they wanted to have lots of adventures when they grew up. They didn't see each other for years until one day, after Dad and Mum had been married for about a year, Sir Wally turned up on the doorstep out of the blue. He told Dad about this island he'd inherited and asked if they were ready for an adventure! He knew that Dad was a doctor and thought that it was important to have a doctor on the island. Mum and Dad thought it might be a bit of a lark and agreed! Now they say that it was a totally mad thing to do, but even so they don't regret it.

'My grandparents are very good and keep the island a secret – I think they tell their friends that Dad is a doctor in the desert, or something! They come out every year to see us. No one else here has visitors except for Sir Wally, so I've no idea whether other people's families know where they are!'

'Does Sir Wally really make all the rules?' asked Gertrude.

'Yes. But he's very good at it so no one minds. He does consult other people sometimes, though. Most of the people here are really good at what they do, and Sir Wally chooses people who he knows will enjoy their work and be happy here.'

'He said something odd about the crew of the cargo boat,' said Hannibal.

'What was that?'

'He said that they don't gossip because they have good reason not to.'

Geoffrey laughed. 'That's because most of them have been in trouble with the law.'

'Really?' asked Tallulah. 'Are they dangerous? That doesn't sound good!'

'Not at all dangerous. Sir Wally told my dad that they were all determined to change their ways and he had managed to get them out of trouble. Sir Wally was an important lawyer back in England. They won't talk because they are so grateful to him. They don't want him to send them back to a place where they had such a rough time.

'Only one of them actually lives on the island – that's Big Bob. You will meet him soon, I'm sure. As well as being our head forester he is a very experienced sailor, so he also helps a lot on the cargo boat which goes between here and Australia occasionally to buy anything that is needed on the island. He's away on the boat at the moment. Most of the crew have been sailors all their lives and have travelled all over the world, so they have some great tales to tell. When the boat is here for a few days they stay with Big Bob in his cabin, but mostly they live in Australia with their families.'

'Listen,' said Hannibal. 'I can hear a horse. Dad must be back.'

The four children rushed out of the kitchen onto the track. Amaryllis was ahead of them and already waiting. Sure enough, along came Quentin and Luke astride the horses.

'So,' Luke said. 'You made it back home.'

'Thanks to you,' said Amaryllis. 'And with a little help from Geoffrey, I gather.'

'With a great deal of help from Geoffrey,' said Quentin. 'It was Geoffrey who got them to the track. We could never have ridden the horses in the tangle of the trees!'

'Come on, Geoffrey,' said Luke. 'Up you get behind me. Let's get you home. Your mum and dad are back, having safely delivered twins – a boy and a girl. Two more residents for our remote island. I promised them that I would get you back home.'

'Wow! Twins!' said Gertrude. 'I guess we'd better start practising a few lullabies!'

'You'll need to practise more than lullabies,' said Luke, as he helped Geoffrey up behind him. 'We've been promised a concert before too long, and you can't start it off by lulling us all to sleep. Though you could finish it that way I guess!'

'Yes, good thinking,' said Geoffrey. 'I'm looking forward to hearing you all play. Good night, everyone. I'll be back tomorrow morning as soon as I've done the hens, then I'll show you round the island.' And Luke and Geoffrey went out into the night.

'Time for bed, I think,' said Amaryllis.

'Yes,' agreed Quentin. 'And I suggest we start thinking about what to perform for our first concert. It appears that we are here for our music so we must all put our thinking caps on! I would like a suggestion from each of you. Choose carefully, and make sure you suggest something for which we have the music. There's no convenient shop selling sheet music for new pieces here!'

Chapter 15

That night, Tallulah lay awake, thinking. What an extraordinary day it had been. And getting lost in the forest – well, that had been particularly disturbing.

She wondered what she might suggest for the first concert but she couldn't think of anything that might appeal to so many people of so many different ages. She tossed and turned as she thought of various possibilities, but none seemed quite right.

When she eventually fell asleep, she had the strangest dream. She dreamt that she was back in the forest with all those tangled banyan trees but none of the others were with her. She was alone and lost and frightened.

The forest was full of strange noises and strange animals. Faces peered round the trunks of every tree, a strange collection of animal faces – animals from all over the world, animals she had seen in the zoo. There were hippos and lions, elephants and kangaroos, giant tortoises and donkeys. The trees were full of multi-coloured birds, piping and whistling, and chattering monkeys were jumping from branch to branch.

It was just as she was dreaming that a kangaroo had leapt at her and knocked her over that she woke up with a start. She was murmuring the words, 'The kangaroo can jump incredible,' and she knew immediately what her suggestion for their first concert would be! That decision made, she grinned, turned over, pulled the blanket up to her chin and fell into a deep sleep.

Everyone slept soundly that night and they were up early, feeling completely refreshed. They were looking forward to Geoffrey's arrival, all of them eager to explore and to learn everything they could about this strange island on the other side of the world.

Geoffrey and Reggie arrived just as they were finishing breakfast.

'Perfect timing,' said Hannibal. 'We're ready to go, unless you want us to help here?'

'No, thank you. Off you go,' said Amaryllis. 'I'll spare you the washing up today. Don't forget to think about the music for our first concert. We'll discuss it this evening, so try to have your suggestions ready. I guessed that you would want to explore today, so I've prepared a picnic to keep you going. It's in this rucksack – you can share the carrying of it. Here, Hannibal, you take the first shift. I've put your bathers in too, in case you find somewhere for a dip. No room for towels so you can run around to get dry. It won't take long in the sun.'

She hoisted the rucksack onto Hannibal's back. 'Have a good time. If you take the rowing boat out, remember to stay close to the shore. And please don't get lost again!'

'Don't worry, Mum,' said Tallulah. 'We've got Geoffrey with us – and Reggie. They know their way around. Thanks for the food.'

'Where are you taking us first, Geoffrey?' asked Hannibal as they reached the top of the zigzag path. 'Down to the beach? We haven't been in the rowing boat yet. Shall we fetch the oars?'

Geoffrey grinned. 'Let's leave the boat for tomorrow. I want to show you the island first. We'll walk round to the other side and I'll show you the lie of the land before we start on the sea!'

'Are we going to walk all the way round? That sounds like a long way. Can we do it in one day?' Tallulah asked.

'We could, easily,' said Geoffrey. 'This is a pretty small island. But we won't walk all the way round today, we'll go about halfway and save the rest for another day. We'll start off along the cliff path, then go down to the beach and have our picnic and a swim in one of the little coves. We can do some shell hunting there – we have the most amazing shells here! Then we'll cut across the island, and up and over the hill to come home. That way, I can show you my very secret place. But you will all have to promise not to tell anyone else about it.'

'Secret place? Where's that? It sounds intriguing.' Gertrude was curious.

'Wait and see,' said Geoffrey. 'I want it to be a surprise. Let's get going. We'll start along the cliff. There's a good path – Sir Wally made sure that there was a path all the way round the island. Sometimes it goes along the cliff top and sometimes it dips down into the bays. Once you're on it, you can't go wrong. It's very easy to follow.'

So began a great day of exploration for the Quintuckles. They set off along the cliff path. Sometimes it sent them scrambling up and down over the rocks, and sometimes along the beaches at the edge of the sea. They all got very hot but they had a refreshing swim before eating their picnic amongst the rocks on one of the many little beaches. They collected curious and beautiful shells which they stowed carefully in the rucksack.

Towards the end of the afternoon, they came across a stream tumbling its way to the sea. 'It will soon be time to head for home,' said Geoffrey. 'But I've been saving the best till last. We're now on our way to my favourite place. Follow me – and watch your step, as it's a bit steep and stony. We're not going back along the coast, we are going up and over!'

He headed into a cleft which the stream had cut through the hill as it hurtled downwards. The water tumbled and sparkled as it flowed swiftly under and over rocks and stones. The children clambered up the rocky hillside following the stream. Almost at the top, high above their heads, was a great hole in the rocks out of which the water was tumbling. It seemed to be singing as it hurtled down in a great curving sheet and made a loud, joyous noise as it plunged over the rocks on its way down to the sea.

It was quite magical. The three Quintuckle children stood and gazed in amazement.

'Golly, I can see why this is your favourite place!' Tallulah had to shout to be heard over the thundering of the water.

'Oh no! We haven't quite reached that yet. Come on. Follow me.'

'Wait a minute. Where's Reggie? He seems to have vanished!'

'Don't worry. He's gone on ahead. He knows where we are heading.'

The Quintuckles followed Geoffrey as he continued to clamber over huge boulders underneath the point where the water emerged from the rocks, then he moved round a big rock and disappeared.

Hannibal was the first to follow him. As he rounded the rock, he saw a narrow gap that Geoffrey was squeezing through. Hannibal followed with Gertrude.

Tallulah had paused to look at a piece of something shiny, almost jewel-like, which was embedded in the top of one of the rocks. When she looked up, the others had completely disappeared. She shouted, but the sound of her voice was lost in the clamour of the water. For a moment she panicked. Wherever had they disappeared to? Had they been swept away by the water? But then Geoffrey appeared from behind the rocks, beckoned to her and led her through the narrow gap between the rocks.

'Wow!' Tallulah exclaimed.

"Wow indeed!" The three Quintuckles were astounded to find themselves on a ledge underneath the hole in the rocks out of which the great arc of water was hurtling. They were both underneath and behind the waterfall – and there was Reggie, jumping up at them and wagging his tail.

The noise of the water tumbling over their heads filled the air. They had to shout their very loudest to be heard.

'This is amazing!' yelled Tallulah.

'Wow!' said Gertrude. 'Incredible.'

'Awesome!' Hannibal was staring at the arc of water above him.

The spray splattered them like rain. They stood for some time, reluctant to move from such magic, but then Geoffrey beckoned them to follow him. He went to the back of the ledge and the Quintuckles followed him into a hole in the rocks.

They found themselves in a small cave. Hardly any daylight filtered through here, and Geoffrey was nowhere to be seen in the gloom.

Suddenly, with a loud 'Boo!' he jumped out at them. Strangely, the sound of the tumbling water was muted in the cave and they could talk more easily.

'This is amazing Geoffrey! However did you manage to find this?' asked Gertrude.

'It was actually Reggie who found it. I was terrified when I saw him disappearing between the rocks. I thought he'd be carried away by the water and dashed to pieces. If I'd stopped to think I would have realised how dangerous it might be to follow him, but I didn't stop to think! And so I discovered this amazing place!'

And what a magical place it was! Geoffrey had made a sort of den in the small cave. There were two folded blankets, both quite dry in spite of the water tumbling over the rocks overhead. He had placed a little store of food on a shelf: dried fruit; a tin of ginger biscuits; a bottle of lemonade, and a tin of liquorice rings.

'Those biscuits look awfully tempting,' said Tallulah. Ginger snaps were a great favourite of hers.

'For emergencies only!' said Geoffrey. 'But you can have one if you are really hungry.'

'Wouldn't dream of it!' said Tallulah. 'Emergency only! But I sincerely hope that there won't ever *be* any emergencies!'

'Very unlikely,' said Geoffrey. 'But you never know! I haven't told anyone else about the cave. I thought it would be fun to have a secret place, a part of the island that even Sir Wally hadn't discovered. I didn't want anyone but me – and of course Reggie – to know about it. But when you three came, I suddenly *did* want to share it! So now it's not *my* secret place, it's *our* secret place!'

'Thank you,' said the Quintuckles in unison.

'Quite wonderful!' said Hannibal.

'Brilliant!' agreed Gertrude.

'Unbelievably amazing!' Tallulah said.

'It can be our secret meeting place,' said Hannibal. 'But we'd better move on, it's getting late. We don't want the grown-ups sending out another search party!'

'It'll be downhill all the way, so it shouldn't take us too long,' said Geoffrey.

They passed Geoffrey's house on the way, but he came on with them to pick up his bicycle. When they arrived at The Music Shack they were delighted to see not only Geoffrey's bicycle but three shiny, new, tough mountain bicycles. Bikes had arrived for the adults too, but they had already been put away in the stables.

The three children decided to try out their bikes and cycled with Geoffrey to his home before returning to The Music Shack. They declared the bikes perfect! Now they would be able to get around the island quickly – even though the rides would be extremely bumpy over the rough roads. They would certainly have to watch out for punctures.

That evening, the children gave an account of their tour of the island – without of course mentioning the secret cave behind the waterfall – and the details of their bumpy cycle ride. Tallulah had fallen off twice but had suffered nothing worse than two scraped knees. Then the subject of the concert was raised once more.

'I hope that you're brimming over with ideas,' said Quentin. 'Remember that we need something that everyone will enjoy, so nothing too highbrow. Neither should it be too difficult for us to play, of course! Let's make a decision tomorrow. We do need to get going. There are only two weeks to our first concert, and we really need to make a good impression!'

Chapter 16

Over breakfast the next morning Quentin said, 'Right! Let's get moving on the concert. I hope that you are all full of ideas. Let's go in order of age, oldest first. We won't make any comments until we've heard everyone's ideas. Now, Ambrose, do you have a suggestion?'

'What about something from Handel's *Water Music*? We've all played it before and it's very pleasant to listen to.' There was a general murmur of approval.

'Good thinking, Ambrose,' said Quentin, writing it down. 'Millicent? You next.'

'I was thinking of *Peter and the Wolf*. That's fun.'

'It certainly is,' said Quentin, 'That was going to be my suggestion too, as it happens.' He added it to the list. 'There's something in that for everyone to enjoy. What about you, Amaryllis?'

'Holst. Something from *The Planets*. It seems

appropriate. At the moment it really does feel as though we've all landed on another planet! But maybe that's a bit too ambitious? We'd have to adapt it to fit our instruments.'

'It certainly would be a challenge,' said Quentin, and he added it to the list. 'But absolutely marvellous if we could pull it off.'

Hannibal and Gertrude had both chosen selections from the *Peer Gynt Suite*. They'd played it in the school orchestra recently, so they knew the music well.

'Yes, good idea,' Quentin said. 'Full of variety. And finally you, Tallulah. I guess you are opting for *Peer Gynt* too, as you've played it recently?'

'No – though I do think it's a good idea. But I'm thinking about that concert we went to in the Albert Hall last Christmas when they played *The Carnival of the Animals* – could we do that?'

Both Hannibal and Gertrude started clapping. 'Oh yes, yes! Great idea. I'd love to have a go at that,' said Gertrude.

'That concert certainly was amazing!' Hannibal said. 'Good thinking, Tallulah! But I'm not sure that we could do it with the instruments that we have.'

'And anyway, have we got the music?' asked Gertrude. 'We've never played it before, and we can't go to a music shop and buy it. Nor can we order it online.'

'I've played it before,' said Amaryllis. 'Several times. It is scored for two pianos and various instruments. Sir

Wally has promised to move the airport piano here – we must remind him. Tallulah, you could have a go at the second piano, though we really need you on the violin, too! I once played in a scaled-down version especially designed for school orchestras. If Sir Wally's men have brought out all our music, as they say they did, there's a good chance that it may be there. It's a shame that we don't have all the instruments we'd need to do the whole thing, but we could certainly do a selection of the pieces and it is great fun. I'll go and see if I can find it.'

A few minutes later, there was a loud knocking on the door of the cabin. 'I'll go,' said Quentin, getting to his feet and heading for the door.

Outside was Geoffrey with his bike. 'I've just come to tell you that Luke is on his way with the horse and cart. He'll be here in a minute. He's bringing the piano from the airport, and he's got Robin and Phil with him. He asked me to come back and ask you to clear a space for it.'

'Oh great! Come on in Geoffrey,' said Quentin. 'We're making plans for our first concert and we were talking about that piano. The others are in the kitchen. Go and fetch them would you, Geoffrey? We'll need everyone's help – moving a grand piano is no picnic!'

Soon everyone was outside. The horse and cart came into view. 'Ah good!' said Luke. 'Many hands make light work! I've brought a ramp and I reckon that we'll manage with everyone's help.'

It took a good bit of heaving and pushing – and many encouraging barks from Reggie – but eventually the piano was on the platform in the concert room. Once it was in place Amaryllis unearthed her piano tuning kit and spent some time working on it. The morning flew by and soon it was time for lunch.

Quentin had found the music for all the suggestions and while they were eating, they discussed the concert again. It was time to make a decision. 'It's time to vote,' said Quentin. 'I think we have a marvellous collection of suggestions here. Let's start with *The Carnival of the Animals*. Hands up for that.

All hands were raised; the vote was a clear victory for Tallulah's choice. The arrival of the second piano and finding the music had been the deciding factors.

'But all the other suggestions are wonderful. We'll save them for another day,' said Quentin. 'Shall we divide the poems between us?'

There was a murmur of agreement, then Tallulah said, 'Wait a minute. I've got a better idea. How about you, Geoffrey? You've certainly got a really big voice – all that shouting in the woods when you heard the horses coming. I'll bet you'd really enjoy taking part.'

'Great idea,' said Quentin. 'How about it, Geoffrey?'

'Oh no! I'd be rubbish at spouting poetry,' Geoffrey protested.

'This is a different sort of poetry,' said Tallulah. 'Listen to this.

"'If you think the elephant preposterous
You've probably never seen a rhinosterous!'"

'And what about this!' said Hannibal.

"'The rooster is a roistering hoodlum
His battle cry is cock-a-doodleum!'"

Gertrude chipped in with:
"'The nightingale sings a lullaby
And the seagulls sing a gullaby.'"

Geoffrey laughed. 'Oh, righto. If it's funny, I'll give it a go.'

'Good lad,' said Quentin. 'I think that we shouldn't try to do too much for our first concert. We don't want to bore our audience. We'll have to play around with the instruments quite a bit, and we know that we can't manage all of the sections, but with a bit of ingenuity we'll be able to cobble something together worth listening to. We'll have a look at it this very afternoon and make a decision on which sections we can perform. Off you go, kids. We'll let you know what we decide.'

'What day is it back in Windleford?' asked Tallulah, as the children made their way towards the beach. 'And what time? I'm losing track.'

'We are twelve hours ahead, according to Sir Wally,' Geoffrey said.

'And what day is it? You must know.'

'Oh, I don't worry about the days,' said Geoffrey. 'They're all much the same to me.'

'I like it here but I do think a lot about home. I miss my friends,' said Tallulah. 'Everyone was planning all sorts of adventures for the holidays. I want to know what they all did.'

'And I was hoping to get into the hockey team this year. Miss Woods told me last term that she thought I had a good chance,' said Gertrude rather glumly.

'I wonder what will happen when none of us turn up,' said Hannibal. 'Do you think that they'll start a search?'

'Your school might, because they'll miss you from the orchestra. I don't think mine will worry. Miss Barrow will be glad I'm out of the way. I'm always in trouble,' said Tallulah. 'The last thing she said to me in her prissy voice was, "Next year will be your last year in this school, Tallulah. You need to work harder and not spend so much time on your music. There will be time for that later. I want you to come back next term prepared to concentrate on your work – and do try to stop daydreaming. You need to be prepared for your senior school!"'

Gertrude and Hannibal laughed. Tallulah had mimicked Miss Barrow's very high, rather posh voice perfectly.

Geoffrey grinned. 'I think I'd rather like to go to school. It sounds like a lot of fun,' he said. 'But let's enjoy where we are. Let's have a swim. I'll race you down to the water.'

In the music room, Ambrose, Quentin and Amaryllis were clearing up the platform. There were still unpacked boxes, which they stacked together at the back.

'Whatever the rights and wrongs of this adventure, you have to admit that this has been a highly efficient kidnap,' said Ambrose. 'Sir Wally gets full marks for organisation and his henchmen get huge plaudits for their skill. It really is a miracle that we – and all the instruments – arrived here in one piece, plus at least half the contents of our house in Sprinton Avenue!'

'Thank goodness you knew where to look for the music, Amaryllis. Let's have a look and see if it is feasible for us to perform.'

After a good deal of discussion, they made a list of what they could manage – with some adaptation!

Introduction: piano
The Royal March of the Lion: piano and trumpet
Cuckoo: piano and clarinet
Hens and Roosters: piano, clarinet and violin
Tortoises: piano, double bass and violin
The Elephant: piano, double bass
Characters with Long Ears (Donkeys): violin
Fossils: all instruments, plus Ambrose on the xylophone
The Swan: piano and cello

'We'll have to start practising straight away.' Quentin was looking at the music. 'This may be a simpler version adapted for the school orchestra, but it's still difficult and we only have two weeks.'

'Right,' said Amaryllis. 'We'll concentrate on the concert for the next two weeks. After that, I must organise the children's schooling. We are here, and it looks as if here we are going to stay for the moment, so we must make the best of it. But it's not going to be easy!'

Chapter 17

The three children, having had their swim, scrambled out of the water. Geoffrey had to go home as he had promised to help his father build a new chicken shed, so he said goodbye. He set off up the zigzag path to collect his bike, with Reggie at his heels.

The others walked along the beach towards the rock pools, stopping now and then to pick up shells. To their surprise, they suddenly heard shouting and furious barking. Geoffrey was running back down the path with Reggie close at his heels. He was pointing out to sea and shouting.

The children couldn't distinguish any words, but Geoffrey was obviously very excited about something – excited and also alarmed. When he reached them he was so out of breath that he could hardly speak. 'Look!' he gasped. 'Look!' He pointed out to sea. 'I spotted it from the top of the cliff. I thought it was passing by. It shouldn't be coming in here.'

The Quintuckle children shaded their eyes against the sun. Coming towards them was a boat, a small, bright-blue cabin cruiser. It was moving swiftly through the water and seemed to be heading straight towards the beach where they were standing. There were four men on the deck.

'It's only a boat,' said Hannibal. 'What's so exciting about that? Do you know whose boat it is, Geoffrey?'

'No, I've never seen it before. It certainly doesn't belong to anyone on the island. It's a motor boat and there are no motor boats on the island, only sail and rowing boats – apart from the cargo boat, of course. It's definitely not one of ours, and it most definitely shouldn't be here!'

'They won't land, will they? Not when they see the notice?' Gertrude asked.

'They shouldn't,' said Geoffrey. 'But they must have already seen the notice and they are still coming – and coming much too fast! Golly! Whatever are they playing at? They're obviously intending to run the boat straight up to your little landing place. Sir Wally will be furious. There are huge warning notices on all the possible landing places on the island.'

He set off at a run towards the oncoming boat, shouting and pointing to the notice and trying to wave the boat away.

At that moment, the Quintuckle children heard

Quentin shouting to them. Turning, they saw him beckoning from the top of the zigzag path. The boat then suddenly veered round and headed away from the beach.

'I should jolly well think so,' said Geoffrey. 'It's a good job your dad appeared because they obviously weren't going to take any notice of us. They must have thought they could deal with a bunch of children! Goodness knows what they thought they were doing. Sir Wally wants to keep the island safe and unpolluted! People either have to sail here or come on the cargo boat. We'd better go and see what your dad wants – and then I'd better head for home or I'll be in trouble!'

Quentin was waiting for them at the top of the path. 'Come on,' he said. 'We've sorted the music. I think we'd better go through it now and make sure that we know which pieces we are able to do with our instruments. Perhaps we'll have time for a preliminary practice before I go to see Sir Wally. There are a few things I need to sort out with him.'

'I'll leave you to it,' said Geoffrey. 'I must go now.'

'Righto, Geoffrey. I'll copy the poems out for you and we'll have a rehearsal as soon as possible.'

'Are you quite sure you want me? I might make a terrible mess of it.'

'Nonsense! It's just a bit of fun,' said Quentin. 'And you won't make a mess of it. You'll be a star! Just enjoy it!'

'Well, if you're sure… I promised to help Dad this

afternoon but I'll come back after that. Happy rehearsing!'
And he was off.

'Right,' said Quentin. 'A quick lunch and then it's down to work.'

Sir Wally had asked if their first concert could be in two weeks' time. He wanted to gather all the island residents to hear the new arrivals' music as soon as possible. He had promised everyone a concert and he wanted to prove that kidnapping the Quintuckles had been worth it.

'Everyone is working so hard to make this island a good place in which to live,' Sir Wally had said. 'But they are not getting any sort of entertainment and I do want their lives to be enjoyable as well as useful and practical.'

That afternoon, the Quintuckles had their first rehearsal. This version of *The Carnival of the Animals* had been scaled down, so it was much simpler and used fewer instruments than the big concert version. Nevertheless, it was quite tricky – though huge fun to play.

The instrument line-up that they eventually settled on was Amaryllis on the piano, Gertrude on the cello, Tallulah on second piano and the violin, Millicent on the clarinet, Quentin on double bass, Hannibal on the flute, and Ambrose on the trumpet and the xylophone. They were just tuning up when Geoffrey arrived. He suddenly appeared and put his hands over his ears as he heard the cacophony of sound. Tuning up can be a very raucous affair, and raucous this certainly was!

Quentin handed Geoffrey the words for *The Royal March of the Lion*. 'Here you are, Geoffrey,' he said. 'Make yourself useful! Have a go. Make it big – big as you like. Make it as loud as you can.'

Geoffrey opened his mouth and read the words in a surprisingly loud and powerful voice that surprised everyone.

"'The lion is the king of beasts,
And husband of the lioness.
Gazelles and things on which he feasts
Address him as Your Highoness.
There are those that admire that roar of his,
In the African jungles and veldts
But I think, wherever a lion is,
I'd rather be somewhere else.'"

When he finished, they all laughed and clapped. Who would have thought that such a huge voice could emerge from so small a body?

'Brilliant,' said Quentin. 'Really great, Geoffrey. You will most certainly make everyone sit up and listen. Right, let's have it again – and this time we'll crash in with the music at the end.'

Geoffrey read out the words in stentorian tones. As he came to the end of the verse, the Quintuckles plunged into the music. They were certainly making a very loud and very joyful sound and Geoffrey started to giggle.

That set them all off, and the music came to a sudden end as they collapsed with laughter.

'Great. A good start,' said Quentin when they had pulled themselves together. 'Now let's get down to serious business. Let's try *Hens and Roosters*. Come on, Millicent, we need you on the clarinet for this one. Off you go, Geoffrey.'

"The rooster is a roistering hoodlum
His battle cry is cock-a-doodleum.
Hands in pockets, cap over eye,
He whistles at pullets passing by."

They laughed a lot as they tried to make animal noises on their instruments; donkeys, cockerels, lions and elephants roamed around The Music Shack that day.

'Golly,' said Geoffrey. 'I didn't know that music could be such a lark!'

The rehearsal continued until Sir Wally suddenly walked into the room unexpectedly. At that moment, Amaryllis on the piano and Gertrude on the cello were playing *The Swan*. Sir Wally stood stock still just inside the door until they had finished playing. There was a moment of silence, then everyone started to clap. 'Absolutely beautiful,' said Sir Wally. 'I don't think that I have ever heard anything so lovely.'

'Good work, everyone,' said Quentin. 'That's enough for today. Time for tea and cake.'

They were certainly ready for that; they had made a good start and *The Carnival of the Animals* was most definitely a lot of fun.

Chapter 18

The next two weeks were a mixture of laughter and hard work. Geoffrey arrived early every morning and all four children went straight down to the beach. They became proficient at handling the little rowing boat, keeping well inside the bay, as they had been told. They swam, they played games in the woods, and Geoffrey taught them some of his tracking skills. They soon had a wonderful and varied collection of shells and pebbles. And wherever they went, whatever they were doing – in or out of the sea – Reggie was always with them, jumping and barking and wagging his tail. He, like them, was having a great time!

The afternoons were spent rehearsing *The Carnival of the Animals*, which was getting better and better with each rehearsal. After each rehearsal they tried to get in a brief swim before Geoffrey had to go home.

Then came an afternoon when the rehearsals finished early. The children were told that they could have a longer spell of freedom while the music room was being prepared for the performance. There were only two days to go before the concert.

They took the boat out and, after rowing around the bay for a while, they had a swim. They stayed in the sea for a long time, and the sun was already setting when they eventually came out of the water. Putting on their sandals and picking up their towels, they headed towards the zigzag path up to the house.

Hannibal turned back to look at the sun setting over the water. The colours of sky and sea were dazzling. 'Oh! Just look at the sunset!' he shouted. 'It's glorious!'

They all turned: the sunset was indeed glorious. Streaks of red and orange and gold swept across the sky.

Geoffrey shaded his eyes and looked out to sea. 'That's funny,' he said. 'Look, there's that motorboat coming towards us again. And I do believe that it's trying to land! Didn't they get the message the first time they came so close? Stupid things!' He set off towards the water at a run, waving his arms and pointing at the PRIVATE ISLAND. STRICTLY NO LANDING notice. The others followed him and waved their arms about too to give Geoffrey some support.

But the boat kept on coming at speed and soon reached the landing stage. One man stayed on it, while three other men jumped out and ran towards the children who were standing open-mouthed in astonishment.

The men didn't look at all friendly – quite the opposite in fact; they looked really threatening. They were total strangers, strangers who were obviously up to no good.

Geoffrey dropped his towel and started running back up the beach towards the cliff path, shouting at the top of his voice. 'Run back to the house! Quickly! Quickly!'

The others dropped their towels and turned to follow him, but they were not quick enough. One man grabbed Hannibal whilst the other grabbed both the girls, holding one under each arm and lifting them off their feet.

Reggie was barking furiously and leaping at the men. They kicked out at him and dragged the three Quintuckles back to the boat where they were thrown in, landing in a tangled heap on the floor. Their towels were thrown in after them.

The third man had set out in pursuit of Geoffrey, who was starting to run up the zigzag path. Geoffrey soon realised that there was absolutely no way that he could make it to the top without being caught. What should he do? His only chance was to try to shake off his pursuer. He must throw himself into one of the thick bushes and try to hide there? No good! His pursuer was too close and would surely see him and drag him back. It was hopeless, and it looked as if Geoffrey would soon be dragged into that boat too.

But he hadn't reckoned on Reggie, who, realising that his master was in trouble, pounded up the path to help him. Just as Geoffrey was rounding one of the zigzags, Reggie grabbed the leg of the man in pursuit, tore a huge piece of material out of the man's jeans and pulled him backwards. The man swore loudly and fell heavily. This gave Geoffrey, who had rounded one of the zigzags and was out of sight of his pursuer for a moment, enough time to throw himself into a thick bush. It was a very painful manoeuvre; not only did he twist his ankle as he hurtled off the path, but the bush turned out to be an exceedingly thorny one.

Somehow Geoffrey managed not to make a sound as the thorns dug painfully into his skin. His pursuer, swearing violently at Reggie and trying to shake him off, continued up the path.

Geoffrey was terribly afraid that Reggie would rush over and reveal his hiding place, but Reggie was much too clever for that. He continued to follow the man, barking furiously and snapping at his heels. A few moments later the man returned, with Reggie still in pursuit. Geoffrey, his heart beating faster than he would have thought possible, kept absolutely still as Reggie chased the stranger down the zigzags and out onto the beach.

Peering cautiously out of the bush, Geoffrey saw that the man was carrying a gun and was racing back across the beach towards the motorboat, with Reggie still in pursuit. The running man was waving his arms about wildly and shouting at the men on the boat. As soon as he reached it, he threw himself aboard, the engine roared and the boat was manoeuvred swiftly and efficiently away from the shore and out to sea.

There was absolutely no sign of the three children, though Geoffrey could see all four men. He thought that he recognised one of the men who had stayed on the boat as someone he knew well, a giant, very much taller and broader than the other three. Surely that was Big Bob? It certainly looked like him but at this distance Geoffrey couldn't be certain. What on earth would Big Bob be doing with these men? No, surely it couldn't be him! He was in Australia with the cargo boat, wasn't he?

There was no sign of the Quintuckle children on board; they must already have been hidden away in the cabin. Within a few moments the boat had rounded the rocks at the far end of the bay and was out of sight. Reggie was still barking furiously and staring out to sea.

Geoffrey crawled from his hiding place and called Reggie, who bounded towards him. Geoffrey made his way as fast as he could up the path. He had to get help – and quickly! He was bleeding from the many scratches he had suffered from the thorny bush and he looked a very sorry sight.

How on earth was he going to break the news to the grown-ups that Gertrude, Hannibal and Tallulah had been kidnapped – yet again? And this time it was quite obvious that the kidnappers had evil intentions because they had been so brutal in the way they had grabbed the children.

Geoffrey didn't think for one moment that the Quintuckle children had been kidnapped for their musical abilities, as had been the case in Windleford. These four kidnappers were undoubtedly quite ruthless. They were obviously after ransom money. They must know that Sir Walter was mega rich. And if they didn't get their money, what then? What then, indeed? Geoffrey shuddered to think what might happen to Gertrude, Hannibal and Tallulah.

Chapter 19

Ambrose, Quentin, Millicent and Amaryllis had been busy putting the music room in order for the concert. The stage was set out with the pianos and chairs, and the music for *The Carnival of the Animals* was on the music stands. Chairs for the audience were arranged in rows.

Quentin was about to go down to the beach to call the children in for lunch when Geoffrey came bursting into the room. They all looked up in astonishment – Geoffrey out of breath, his face and body covered in blood.

'Geoffrey!' said Millicent. 'Good gracious! Whatever has happened to you? You'd better come into the kitchen so that we can clean you up and put some dressings on those cuts and scratches. What have you been up to? And where are the others?'

'Kidnapped!' gasped Geoffrey.

There was a moment's startled silence.

'Kidnapped?' Ambrose, Millicent, Quentin and Amaryllis repeated in unison.

'Whatever do you mean, Geoffrey?' asked Quentin.

'We have to tell Sir Wally,' said Geoffrey. 'He will know what to do. They were grabbed on the beach by four men and taken away in a boat. One of the men had a gun, so he is certainly not one of our islanders!'

For a few moments there was a stunned silence as the four grown-ups stared at Geoffrey. Not more kidnapping, surely! This was unbelievable. It was not very long ago that they'd been kidnapped and brought to this island, and they'd only just started to accept the situation. Was it even remotely possible that the children had been kidnapped again? Surely not! Geoffrey must surely be mistaken. They stood, open-mouthed, staring at him in disbelief.

Faced with a similar situation in England, they would have called in the police immediately, and within minutes there would have been people out searching with dogs and radios to help them. But there was no such help here. Whatever should they do now?

It was Geoffrey who eventually broke the silence. 'I'll cycle round to Sir Wally's house. He'll know what to do.'

'Will he be there?' Quentin asked. 'He could be anywhere on the island.'

'Don't worry. He should be there at this time of day, and if he isn't then Peter will know where to find him.'

'Good plan, Geoffrey. Thank you. But why don't I fetch Sir Wally while you go and tell your parents what has happened? Perhaps you could bring them back here and the three of you could help us make some sort of plan.'

'Good thinking. I'm quite sure that they'll want to help,' said Geoffrey. 'You go for Sir Wally and I'll find my mum and dad, then we'll all meet back here!'

'What did these men look like, Geoffrey? Do you think that they will hurt the children?' Amaryllis could hardly speak, and her words came out in a whisper.

'The man who stayed on the boat looked like Big Bob who lives on the other side of the island. But I can't believe that he would do anything like this. He's usually so jolly! He had his back to me, but he stands out because he is so enormously tall. But I don't think that it could have been him. As for the others, I've certainly never seen them before. They were strangers. They definitely don't live here, and they didn't look like natives of the islands. Most probably they're Australians or New Zealanders – and they'll almost certainly be after ransom money.'

'So it will be in their interest to keep their hostages safe,' said Quentin. 'If that is so, they won't hurt the children.' He was trying hard to reassure Amaryllis, but his voice trembled as he spoke. 'Who exactly *is* Big Bob? What does he do here?'

'He's one of the woodsmen. He lives on the other side of the island,' said Geoffrey. 'He's an Australian. He also organises the cargo ship sailings and looks after the crew when they are here. He's different from most of the people here – he's a big strong chap, but not particularly fond of company and keeps very much to himself. My mum and dad think that he's just shy really.

'When you get him to talk, he seems really nice! We call him one of Sir Wally's experiments! There are several of those around on the island. Sir Wally likes to collect up people who have not had many advantages in life, as well as people like medical workers and musicians. You haven't met Big Bob yet because he's been away. He went on the cargo boat to Australia a few days ago. He had a lot of work to do there for Sir Wally, buying new equipment. I didn't think that Big Bob was due back yet, but I suppose it's possible that the boat has come back earlier than expected.'

'We'll talk to Sir Wally about him,' said Quentin. 'We must try to stay positive. Come along, Geoffrey, there's no time to lose. Let's get our bikes then you can go and find your parents and I'll find Sir Wally. Hurry! The sooner we get help the better!'

Quentin and Geoffrey were soon speeding away from The Music Shack in different directions on their bicycles. Quentin was anxious to speak to Sir Wally and pedalled as fast as he could to Sir Wally's cabin. He was very much out of breath when he arrived and banged loudly on the door.

Marina opened it and, seeing his distress, led him straight through to the office. Quentin told Sir Wally what had happened to the children, and very soon they were both cycling back to The Music Shack.

Chapter 20

The Quintuckle children had been thrown roughly into the tiny cabin on the boat. Their towels were thrown in after them. Lying together in a heap on the floor, they heard the key being turned in the lock: they had been imprisoned.

There was no light in the cabin, only a dim lifting of the darkness thanks to a tiny pane of dirty glass in the top of the door. Everything had happened so quickly that the children couldn't think straight. Whatever was going on? One moment they had been merrily splashing about in the sea, and now here they were, on the floor of a tiny cabin in the gloom, locked in and heading rapidly away from the island.

They banged on the door and demanded to be let out.

'Shut up or you'll be sorry!' was the only answer they got. 'And get some clothes on! There are some on the bunk!'

The children were shocked into silence. The only sound was the throbbing of the engine.

This was far, far worse than their kidnap from Sprinton Avenue. This time they were on their own, on the opposite side of the world from their home in England. And this time they didn't have the grown-ups with them for reassurance.

Slowly, they picked themselves up off the floor and perched side by side on the single bunk. Tallulah was fighting back the tears, Gertrude was valiantly trying to comfort her by throwing her arms around her, and Hannibal's brain was in a whirl, his mind full of questions. Why had these men grabbed them off the beach? How on earth did they know they were there? Had they been keeping a look-out for them? What use could three children be to them? What should they do now? How could they escape?

As their eyes accustomed to the gloom, they noticed a pile of clothes on the bunk.

'Let's get dressed and make a plan,' said Hannibal.

'I'm not wearing any of those!' said Gertrude. 'They look disgusting, and they won't fit. They're all huge!'

'We don't have a choice,' said Tallulah. 'We can't just wear our bathers!'

At least their swimsuits were now fairly dry, so they pulled an odd assortment of clothes on over them. The sweaters were huge and garishly horrible, and the children looked decidedly peculiar, but at least they were covered up.

They could hear the men talking and laughing outside. The engine noise made it difficult to hear what they were saying, but the children picked out a few odd words: 'good work, mate' and 'look what that ruddy dog has done to my daks' and 'the boss is going to be well pleased'. The children recognised some of the words they spoke as Australian slang: 'fair dinkum', 'boss', 'cobber' and 'drongo'.

'Just listen to them,' said Gertrude. 'We've been kidnapped by some Australian crooks.'

'Yes, for a ransom, no doubt!' said Hannibal.

'Don't be silly! Who is going to pay them? Mum and Dad don't have much – only the collection from Saturday's busking. And they can't exactly nip to the bank in Windleford and get some money out, can they? Come to think of it, nobody uses money here, so what's the point of demanding it?' Tallulah was getting over the shock of being kidnapped for a second time and was trying to get her thoughts together.

'It's probably only our island that has a sort of barter system instead of using money,' Hannibal pointed out. 'I expect that most of these islands are expensive holiday places. The people on those will certainly use money – lots and lots of it!'

'Let's try and talk to these men,' said Tallulah. 'If we tell them that they can't get any ransom money out of our parents, perhaps we can persuade them to take us back to the island.'

'No chance,' Hannibal said. 'Think about it. They wouldn't have gone to all this trouble to capture us without knowing there's a jolly good chance of getting whatever they're after! I'm quite sure that they are relying on Sir Wally for money. These people must know that he is mega-mega rich! And they don't care tuppence about us – they'd probably rather throw us overboard than take us back.'

There was a glum silence as the three children considered this awful thought.

'I still think it's worth a try,' said Tallulah, and she started beating on the door. 'Let us out!' she shouted. 'We want to talk to you.'

'Well, we don't want to talk to you. Shut your trap or you'll be sorry!' replied a harsh voice.

They sat gloomily on the bunk. The boat moved on, taking them further and further away from the island. Then, after a while, there was a sudden silence: the engine noise had ceased abruptly. The boat slowed and stopped, bobbing up and down on the waves. The four men stopped talking for a few moments, then started to quarrel violently, their voices getting louder.

With the engine silenced, the children could hear them clearly. One of the men, who was obviously the leader, had a very rough, gravelly voice and he did most of the talking. They were having a row about what to do with the children. It seemed that they had arrived at their intended destination – a small private island – expecting it to be deserted; now they were furious to find that there were lots of people enjoying themselves. There were people on the beach and swimming in the sea, and the children could hear the sounds of music and laughter which were carried over the water.

From what their kidnappers were now saying, it was apparent that the original plan had been to hide the children there until a ransom had been secured. This was no longer possible. Most inconveniently for the kidnappers, the owners must have arrived unexpectedly with lots of guests. So what was to be done now? Where could they hide the children and who was going to guard them until the men got their money?

'You're the one who knows the area, Bob,' said one of them. 'You must know somewhere where we can hide them away until we get the ransom money?'

'Let me think,' Bob said, very loudly and slowly. 'I suppose I could take you to Zeci Island – it's not far away from here. It's basically uninhabited, but I've got an old pal who has a remote cabin there. He may or may not be there, but it would make the ideal hiding place for the kids. If my pal is there, we can give him some of the ransom money. I'm sure he'll be only too anxious to help. Pedro will do anything for money.'

'And if he's not there, what then?'

'Then we'll have to think again. We'll find a way. I'm sure Sir Wally will cough up the money very quickly and the children will soon be rescued. And you will have your money, and everyone will be happy!'

'Zeci? Never heard of it, but there are so many private islands around here! It sounds like an idea. Can you get us there? And can we get in there with this boat?'

'That's another advantage,' Bob said. 'I know a good landing place. I've done a fair bit of fishing around here. The chap who owns the island has a cabin with a decent landing stage but, according to Pedro, he's hardly ever there. Pedro goes there quite a lot to keep an eye on the place for the owner. Of course, if we find a super yacht at the jetty and the owner *is* there, we won't be able to land. But it's surely worth a try, isn't it?'

'And what if your pal Pedro isn't there? Can we get into his cabin?'

'No problem,' Bob replied. 'There's nothing in there to steal. I don't think Pedro keeps it locked and, even if he does, we're all pretty good at breaking locks, aren't we!'

'You're sure you can find this cabin?'

'Well, Zeci is just a hill rising out of the sea like so many of the little islands around here. It's probably volcanic. Wherever we land, we just keep climbing. I think that I can find the cabin fairly easily, it's up on the top of the hill. But I've not been there for a long time so I suggest that we leave the children locked in here while we do a recce. They'll be a nuisance until we know exactly where we're taking them. Of course, if Pedro's not there then one of us will have to stay on the island with the kids until we get the ransom money. I'll stay with them myself, if you like.'

'Oh no, you won't! We need you to guide us round these islands and you're far better at handling the boat than we are. That's the only reason we pulled you in on this job! Now you've got to earn your cut! Okay, take us to Zeci and be quick about it. We need to get this sorted fast. Will your friend's boat be at the jetty if he's there?'

'Possibly, but unlikely. It's very small. He usually just pulls it onto the beach nearest his cabin.'

The engine started up; they were moving again. Hannibal got off the bunk and put his eye to the grubby bit of glass in the cabin door. He had a fairly good view of one of the men, who was at the helm of the boat. It was the very big man who had been waiting on the boat when they were snatched off the beach. So he was the one they called Bob, thought Hannibal. Could he be the Big Bob that Geoffrey had talked about when they visited the woodcutters? He certainly was huge, a giant of a man with a big powerful body.

The four men stopped arguing and lapsed into silence. Maybe they were asleep and Bob, at the wheel, was the only one awake.

The three Quintuckles sat despondently side by side on the bunk. They were brave children, but all that they could think of at that moment was that with every minute the boat was taking them further and further away from their island, away from The Music Shack, away from their family. As it moved steadily on through the water, the only sound now was the monotonous drone of the engine.

Quite suddenly, the engine made a coughing noise and stopped. For a moment there was total silence and then a shout. Bob's voice. 'Hey! Wake up you lot! We're here! This is Zeci.'

'Where? All I can see is water!'

'You're looking the wrong way, you idiot. Look – land! And there is the landing stage. We just need to go alongside and tie up. The owner's cabin is over there and there is no boat and no lights on, so no one is in residence. The coast is clear. We'll be quite safe. And if by a remote chance the owner suddenly turns up while we're here – which is extremely unlikely – we'll just say that we are overnighting here and moving on in the morning. Lots of folk do that round these islands. Come on, let's get a move on. We need to hide these kids till we get the ransom money. We'll give Pedro a cut if he's here – like I told you, he'll do anything for a bit of cash!'

'And what if he's not here?' asked one of the men.

'Too bad. If the worst comes to the worst we'll just dump the kids and go!' said another.

'We can't do that – they might never be found!'

'Of course they'll be found! Stop arguing! Let's go. It'll be getting dark soon and we won't be able to see where we're going. You can bet your life that Sir Wally will soon be on the warpath and scouring the islands. And if he catches us, there will be no ransom money and we'll very likely find ourselves back in prison! Maybe we *should* just dump the kids here and get away.'

'Are you mad? This kidnap could give us enough money to set us up for life! Sir Wally is mega-rich by all accounts! I'm not giving up now after all the risks we've taken to get this far.'

They started shouting at each other until one of them shouted, 'Listen to me. Let's lock the kids in here and do our recce. Let's find this hut first. If we find it, we can come back for the children. If this Pedro is there, he'll know what's best to do.'

'And if he's not there?'

'As I said before – we'll dump the kids and go.'

'What if they starve to death?'

'We won't let that happen. Once the money comes in, we'll let people know where they are. If the worst comes to the worst and Sir Wally refuses to pay up, we'll let the police know where they can find the kids. Come on! We're wasting precious time. We need to get going.'

'Fine,' said Bob. But before we go, let's check that the cabin door is secure. We don't want our hostages to escape.'

'Good thinking, Bob. You're supposed to be a bit of a mechanic, so you see to it. Make sure that door is properly secure.'

'Okay.'

There was a rattling at the door lock and a banging on

the door and a deep voice shouting loudly: Bob's voice. 'We're off now. We won't be gone for very long, so don't try any funny business. You'll never get through that door. I pride myself on my security skills – I've had a lot of practise! They may have landed me in prison, but they've also made me a lot of money.'

'Come on, Bob!' yelled an irritated voice.

'I won't be a minute, I'll just give the lock an extra special twist just to make absolutely sure. You carry on and I'll catch you up.' There was more scraping followed by a banging on the door as Bob shouted, 'Listen to me, you kids. There is absolutely no point in trying to escape! Of course, you can try it if you like – don't let me stop you – but you will be wasting your time and energy. We're off to find a nice cosy cabin for you to stay in. Cheerio!'

'You can bet your life we'll try,' muttered Hannibal. 'You might have a surprise when you come back and find us gone!'

There was the sound of retreating footsteps across the deck and then there was nothing but silence. The children were alone.

Chapter 21

'We'll give them a few minutes to get well away, then we'll have a go at this door,' said Hannibal. He was fiddling with the lock. 'I reckon I should be able to pick this – it's not a complicated one. But goodness knows what that Bob fellow has done to it. He sounded pretty certain that the lock is completely secure. I need something long and thin. Any suggestions?'

'I can't think of anything,' said Gertrude. 'Let's have a look round, though it's difficult to see *anything* in here. It'll be more like a feel around than a look around.'

'There must be a light in here somewhere.'

'If you find one, don't turn it on,' warned Hannibal. 'We don't want to draw their attention. We want them to think that we are helpless. We don't want them to return and see what we are up to.'

The three children started to hunt for anything that

might help, peering through the gloom and feeling their way around.

'Here's a drawer with cutlery in it. Let's look there first,' said Tallulah.

'I've found a pile of papers.' said Gertrude. 'Maybe there's a pen near it.'

'Here's a corkscrew,' Tallulah shouted triumphantly.

'Here's a paper clip!' Gertrude said.

'Give them to me,' said Hannibal. He straightened the paper clip, inserted it into the keyhole, twisted and turned it. To their surprise when he rattled the handle, there was a click and the door opened immediately.

'That's funny,' said Hannibal. 'I think that Bob must have made a mistake and *released* the lock instead of making it more secure. He's not as competent as he thinks he is. Won't he be mad when he finds us gone? Let's hang on a minute or two to let the men get clear, then we'll get out of this prison. We have to find somewhere safe to hide!

They waited for a few minutes. 'Okay, come on!' Hannibal said. 'Let's move!'

It was a huge relief to be out of the stuffy cabin and in the fresh air. It was an easy jump from the boat onto the jetty.

Although the sun was now very low in the sky and the light was fading, the children caught a glimpse of Bob before he disappeared behind a rock. The other men were out of sight; they must be ahead of him.

'We'll wait behind this bollard thing until they've gone, then we'll get as far away from the boat as possible,' said Hannibal.

After a few minutes, the children crept across the jetty. The cabin was at the end of it; it was all in darkness but should they knock just in case there was someone there who might help them? Yes. It was definitely worth a try.

They inched across the rough ground to the door of the cabin and knocked quietly. There was no response. They tried again, a little louder, but were again met with silence. There was to be no help from the cabin, so now they needed to get as far away from the boat as possible.

They could still hear the distant voices of their captors as they climbed the steep slope of the hill. Maybe the children's best bet was to go along the shoreline. There seemed to be a rough path, but there were no trees, nowhere to hide should the men see them and come after them.

'We'll have to go uphill where there are bushes and rocks where we can hide,' whispered Gertrude. 'But there seems to be only one track and those men are on it. We certainly don't want to follow them! We'll have to scramble up the hillside as best we can and hope to find somewhere to hide until they stop looking for us and go away.'

'And what do we do then?' whispered Tallulah.

'Goodness knows!' muttered Hannibal. 'We'll just have to hope that the owner of the island visits his cabin before we starve to death. One thing at a time! Let's concentrate on getting away from the boat and finding somewhere to hide. And no talking! Sound carries a long way.'

They scrambled up the rough, steep hill which was scattered with rocks of all sizes. It was hard going but it was wonderful to be out of that locked cabin and free on the hill. They kept close together, talking in whispers.

One of Tallulah's hair ribbons caught on a sharp piece of rock and was dragged off. Her long hair fell about her face. 'Hold on a minute,' she whispered. 'I've lost one of my hair ribbons.'

'No,' whispered Hannibal. 'We can't stop, Tally. Come on. No time to find it now. You've got plenty more at home – and you've still got one ribbon. Tie all your hair back with that. We must keep moving. We need to get as far away from the shore as possible. No more talking. Voices carry a long way, remember! And we *must* stay together so keep close behind me. Any time now, those men might return to the boat. When they find us gone, they'll be on our trail in no time.'

Huge boulders got in their way, some of which they could get round but many of which they had to climb over. It was tough going, and soon they were all out of breath.

As they neared the top of the hill, the three children heard angry voices: the men were coming back down the hill and making their way back to the boat. The children crouched behind a rock and stayed absolutely still.

The voices got nearer and nearer.

'What a waste of time!' the children heard one of the men say. So much for your plan, Bob! You can't even find the flaming hut!'

The voices got quieter as the men continued past the children's hiding place and headed for the quayside.

When they boarded the boat, they would find their captives gone and then they would start searching for them. The three children needed to get as far away as possible. They tried to speed up but the steepness of the climb meant that they didn't have much success.

Back at the boat a fierce argument was raging. 'I thought you said that you'd fixed the lock, Bob,' one of the men said.

'I did my best.'

'Your best wasn't good enough, was it? And now you say that perhaps this isn't Zeci, after all. You've got us lost and you have no idea where we are. You took us up the mountain to find your pal's hut and all we found was a pile of stones. You better think again! You're the one who is supposed to know these islands! And now we find that you can't even lock a door! And the kids are gone. We have to find them – and fast!'

'I'm sorry,' Bob replied. 'There's something the matter with this old tub you hired! The navigating equipment is all to pot. It can't be helped. We'd better make a quick getaway.'

'A getaway? Are you mad? We're not giving up now.

Let's get after those kids and *then* we'll make our getaway – with *them*! They can't have gone far. I'll wave the gun at them – that should keep them in order!'

Hannibal had been quite right about voices carrying. Although the three children couldn't make out what the men were actually saying, it was obvious that their kidnappers had left the boat and were now climbing up the hill again in search of the children – and they were getting closer!

There was a sudden shout from one of the men. He was close enough now for the children to make out the words. 'Hey, look what I've found! We're on the right track. This is that littlest kid's hair ribbon. You can't mistake that bright red. They can't be far away.'

He raised his voice and shouted. 'Okay kids. We're coming to get you. We know which way you've gone. You shouldn't leave your ribbons around! Very silly! We're on our way and we'll soon find you! You might as well give up now.'

Chapter 22

'Come on,' whispered Hannibal. 'Keep moving. We're nearly at the top and we must find somewhere to hide. There are plenty of rocks around.'

'But they won't give up. We need to get as far away as possible,' whispered Gertrude. 'We must keep going – we have to stay ahead of them.'

'I'm not sure I can keep up this pace much longer.' Tallulah was feeling very tired. 'My legs aren't as long as yours and one of my sandals has come undone. I must stop for just a moment and do it up or I'll lose it, then I won't be able to walk at all on this rough ground. Let's get behind this rock.'

'Hurry up,' whispered Gertrude. They huddled together in a little space amongst the rocks while Tallulah fixed her sandal.

'Okay,' she whispered. 'I've fixed it. Let's move on.'

As Tallulah moved out of the shelter of the rocks, to her horror she found that she was gazing at one of the men who was searching amongst the boulders. It was the giant of a man they called Bob, the one who had tried to secure the door of the cabin.

Tallulah turned quickly and pushed the others back into the shelter of the rocks, putting her finger to her lips to warn them not to say anything. Surely Bob must have seen her – he'd seemed to look straight into her eyes! But there was no shout of triumph.

The big man's next words seemed to confirm this. He was very close by. 'Boys! We've got them! I see them!'

'Where?' one of the other men shouted.

'There they are, over to the right. Going up the slope.'

'I don't see them!'

'There! See? They're amongst the rocks over there. They must have crossed over to that side of the hill. Can't you see them moving? We need to cross over to the other slope. Follow me.'

'Are you absolutely sure? I can't see anyone!'

'I'm not *absolutely* sure that it's them – it may be a couple of sheep! It's getting dark so I may be mistaken, but something or someone is definitely moving about over there, and I think it's those kids. It's worth taking a look. I've got very good eyesight and I'm pretty sure I saw one of them disappearing behind that big rock over there. We're going the wrong way. Follow me. We'll soon catch them up.'

'I don't see them, but if you're sure…'

'I can't see them now. They're obviously trying to hide amongst the rocks. Come on! We're wasting time. Let's go before we lose them!'

'Okay, kids,' the men shouted. 'No use hiding. We're coming to get you! It's back to the boat for you!' Gradually their voices sounded more and more distant.

'That was a lucky escape. I was *sure* that he'd seen me,' whispered Tallulah. 'He looked straight at me but then he suddenly turned and looked the other way! The shadow of the rocks must have hidden me.'

'It must have been sheep he saw over there – or the breeze moving the bushes perhaps,' Hannibal muttered. 'They're going in the wrong direction now, but they'll soon discover their mistake and be back on our trail. We have absolutely no idea which direction to go in. At least it will soon be quite dark so it will be harder for them to spot us. We need to find somewhere to hide for long enough to make them give up. Let's move further in amongst these rocks.'

'Listen,' murmured Tallulah. 'I can hear water. It sounds like a waterfall, like the one on our island.'

'You're right, Tallulah,' Gertrude said. 'It *does* sound like a waterfall, but these islands have waterfalls galore. Hey! look at those rocks over there. They look familiar somehow! It couldn't be our waterfall, could it? This couldn't possibly be *our* island? Do you think the boat could have been going round in circles and we've landed on the other side of our own island?'

'Don't be silly!' whispered Hannibal. 'We were in that boat for absolutely ages. We must be miles away from our island. Anyway, you heard them say that this is Zeci and our island is called Hilahila. Come on, we absolutely must keep moving.'

'But you said yourself that the kidnappers are incompetent,' Gertrude objected. 'Maybe the boat *has* been going round in circles. We could be anywhere!'

The noise of the tumbling water got louder and suddenly, as the three children rounded a huge rock, they saw a huge waterfall – a waterfall that they thought they recognised! The water was thundering so loudly that the children had to speak into each other's ears.

'I truly believe that this is our waterfall, and that this is our island!' said Tallulah. 'Quick! If I'm right, we can find that entrance in the rocks and get into Geoffrey's secret place behind the waterfall. They'll never find us there! And even if they knew where we were, they're probably too big to scramble through that gap in the rocks.'

'Can you remember where the entrance is?' asked Hannibal. 'It looks so different in the moonlight and there are so many rocks. I don't know which to go round first. Anyway, I'm not convinced that this *is* our island. There are so many islands and they probably all look pretty much the same!'

Gertrude ignored him. 'I think it's over there.' She pointed and moved towards a large rock.

'No.' Tallulah shook her head. 'Not that one.' Her sharp eyes had spotted something she recognised, the piece of shiny stone embedded in the rock that she had noticed on their first visit to the waterfall. 'Stop, Gertie! It's not that one! Follow me. I promise I know the way. Come on! I can hear those men moving back this way – they must have realised that they are on the wrong track. There's no time to waste! We must hide quickly.'

It was true that the men were now heading their way. Their voices were getting louder. Gertrude and Hannibal had no choice but to follow Tallulah and hope that she was right.

As they squeezed their way through the rocks, the noise of the water rushing over the stones drowned out the shouting of the kidnappers. The three children moved past the rock with the shiny stone. It did indeed hide the entrance. They really were at Geoffrey's secret place! And very soon they were safely hidden under the waterfall. Tallulah's shiny stone had saved them, at least for the moment!

Out on the mountain there was still a little warmth after a day of hot sun, but it was distinctly chilly behind the waterfall. They were glad of their garish sweaters. It was also slightly quieter but, even so, they could hear nothing over the sound of the water.

Hannibal put his finger to his lips to warn them not to speak; if their pursuers knew where they were they might just wait for them to emerge. After all, they couldn't stay there for ever! The children had no idea where the four men were. Perhaps they had assumed that the Quintuckles had started on the descent down the other side of the mountain and were heading off to look for them there. Or perhaps they were still searching among the many rocks around the waterfall. Would they give up, go back to the boat and leave the island? Probably not. After all the difficulties of the kidnap, they surely wouldn't want to say goodbye to the ransom money they hoped for, unless they had no choice.

The children had no intention of moving out of their hiding place until they were quite sure that the danger was past. They certainly couldn't be sure of finding their way back to The Music Shack until daylight so they would have to stay where they were for the time being.

It was almost dark behind the waterfall and it was cold, so cold. And so wet! Water was dripping onto them from the cracks in the rocky roof.

Hannibal beckoned to the two girls and pointed out the entrance to the little cave in the rocks that Geoffrey had shown them on their first visit. He crawled into the cave and the others followed him. As they crept in, Gertrude tripped over Geoffrey's blankets and cushion. Wonderful – just what they needed! It was also much quieter in the little cave, and they could talk freely. The rush of water outside would drown their voices. For the first time, they felt safe.

Huddled together, one blanket underneath them and

one covering them, Tallulah remembered Geoffrey's little store of provisions on the rock shelf. She felt her way across the cave and came back with the bottle of lemonade, the tin of biscuits, the bag of dried fruit and some liquorice rings. Having no idea how long it would be before they dare venture out, they rationed themselves to two ginger biscuits each, plus a handful of raisins, but even that small amount of sustenance tasted delicious and cheered them up. They saved the lemonade and liquorice rings for later. There was plenty of water splashing down, so there was certainly no danger that they would suffer from thirst!

In a little while, despite their predicament and the hardness of the rock beneath the blanket, they were so tired that, one by one, they drifted into an uneasy sleep.

Meanwhile, what was happening out on the mountain? Big Bob – for of course it was Big Bob – knew exactly where he was. He had told the other men that he'd spotted something on the other side of the valley and led them away from where the children were hiding. The men spent some time searching around the rocks on the other side of the valley before they eventually gave up.

'There must be something wrong with your eyesight, Bob,' grumbled one of men. 'But it's getting dark now and they can't get off the island, so we'll be sure to find them in the morning. Let's just go back to the boat now.'

'You go back if you like,' Bob said. 'I'm not giving up yet. I'll stay on watch. Let me have the gun. If the kids emerge from their hiding place, I'll have no trouble bringing them back to the boat if I have a gun in my hand.'

'Please yourself. If you really want to sit here all night, here's the gun.'

'Is it loaded?' asked Bob.

'Of course it's loaded. What's the point of a gun if it isn't loaded? Don't stay too long, though. We need to get away from here as soon as it's light, with or without the children! We'll go without you, if we have to.'

'You'll probably get lost if you do.'

The gun was handed over to Big Bob and the three men set off towards the boat. Big Bob watched them until they were out of sight then he carefully unloaded the gun – he certainly didn't want to risk an accidental shooting – and moved towards the waterfall. He went to the place where he had spotted Tallulah and sat down on the grass with his back against a rock. The moon was rising. It was almost full and gave a good light. Bob felt sure that he would spot the children if they emerged from their hiding place.

He tried his very best to stay awake but, lulled by the sound of the waterfall, he soon drifted into an uneasy sleep. It was several hours later and already getting light when he was roused by the barking of a dog. From his vantage point, Bob could see an animal sniffing around the boulders.

He knew straight away that it was Reggie. Whatever was he doing up here? Bob watched as Reggie sniffed around, but then the dog suddenly disappeared among the wilderness of rocks. Bob thought that he caught the echo of an excited bark, but the clamour of the waterfall was so loud that it drowned out almost every other sound.

Bob couldn't imagine why Reggie was up here at this early hour of the morning, but he was sure that it must be something to do with the children. He waited for the dog to reappear, curious to see what he would do next.

First, however, it was vital that he must get the kidnappers away from the island as quickly as possible. He certainly did not want them to discover that he had deceived them, that he had taken them not to the island they had asked for but to one that he knew would be full of people. He had taken them back, by a roundabout route, to Hilahila instead of taking them to Zeci!

It was very much easier scrambling down the mountain than clambering up it, and Bob was soon within sight of the jetty. To his surprise, the boat was not moored any more – it was moving away from the shore!

The kidnappers were giving up. They had managed to get the engine going and were already well away from the shore. The men on board saw Big Bob coming but they didn't stop, they just waved dismissively and moved out to sea. They had given up hope of ransom money and were now intent on saving their own skins. They obviously thought nothing about abandoning him on what was, as far as they knew, a totally deserted island.

Good riddance to them, thought Bob. Little did they know that, by leaving, they had actually done him a good turn. But he did wonder where they would eventually end up; they were inexperienced sailors and didn't know the area at all!

Big Bob started walking along the shore towards the wharf and the cabin. This was, of course, the cabin in which he lived, usually by himself but sometimes with the cargo boat crew. He was deep in thought. How on earth had he been dragged into this preposterous plot? He thought that he had put his former life of crime behind him. Well, at least he was out of it now, and he never wanted to get involved with any sort of crime again.

What a relief it was to get into his own home. He unloaded the gun and put it away safely in a cupboard. Later on, he would hand it over to Sir Wally who would deal with it. He put the kettle on and made some coffee.

He started to worry about the children. He doubted that they would recognise where they were; they had probably never been on this side of the island before. Would they realise that this was actually their island? Would they find their way home? They must be cold and frightened among those rocks on the mountain top, Bob thought, and probably soaking wet with the spray from the waterfall. But at least they would be safe.

He decided to go back up the mountain and keep watch. Somehow he would make sure that they got home safely and then he would confess everything to Sir Wally. He would explain how he had been dragged into the kidnapping plot.

Taking a rug with him, Big Bob left his cosy cabin and clambered back up the mountain to a spot where he could see the jumble of rocks through which the children had disappeared. He had a clear view of the rocks and the waterfall, and he would certainly see the children if they emerged from wherever they were hiding. But after all his activity in the last few hours, he was desperately tired. Despite his intention to keep watch, Bob drifted into an uneasy sleep.

Chapter 23

You are probably wondering how Reggie came to be up there on the mountain, so let's go back a little and find out. It happened like this.

After Geoffrey's announcement that the Quintuckle children had been snatched from the beach, Quentin leapt onto his bicycle and pedalled off to find Wally to get his advice.

Ambrose, Amaryllis and Millicent were desperately worried and afraid as they waited anxiously for Quentin to return with Wally. At last the two men arrived back at The Music Shack, bringing Peter and Marina with them. Geoffrey also returned, accompanied by his parents, Tom and Joyce.

Reggie was lying on the floor with his head on Geoffrey's feet; he seemed to sense that Geoffrey needed comforting. Everyone was trying to make some sort of sense of what had happened and they were all asking the same question: what was the best thing to do now? They had absolutely no idea where the children might have been taken. Geoffrey had seen the boat heading out to sea, but it had quickly disappeared behind the headland and he had no idea of the direction it had taken after that.

Geoffrey told them that he thought Big Bob was in the boat.

'Oh no,' Wally said. 'It can't possibly have been Big Bob. He's gone to Australia to exchange some of our wood for building materials, and then he has other business to deal with. He won't be back for another few days. As soon as the cargo boat docks, he will report to me and bring the crew with him. That should be in a couple of days' time. We always have a bit of a party! It really can't have been Big Bob that you saw.

'Try not to worry too much. I'm sure that there will be a demand for money very soon and then the children will be returned. It will not be in the kidnappers' interest to harm their hostages. I will pay what they demand. As soon as the children are back safely, we will do our best to bring those men to justice.'

'I still believe that it was Big Bob that I saw. Maybe he met some of his old pals in Australia,' said Geoffrey. 'Maybe they persuaded him to help them and he abandoned the cargo boat.'

'It is true that Big Bob has been in trouble in the past

and did have quite a long spell in prison before I invited him to live here. But we have talked together a great deal and I trust him. He's had a raw deal in life – he was brought up in an orphanage and got mixed up with a gang of criminals whilst in his teens. But he assured me that he regretted his behaviour and wanted to start again, to go straight, and I believed him. I feel sure that he meant it. He has settled down really well on the island. He is very knowledgeable about timber, he is an excellent worker, and he is at last beginning to make friends.

'But if that really was Big Bob that you saw, Geoffrey, no doubt he has been contacted by some of his old cell mates. Perhaps the possibility of making a lot of money *has* tempted him back to his old ways. But I hope that you are mistaken. Perhaps you saw someone who bore a resemblance to Bob. You only saw him from a distance.

'Maybe we should see if we can find him. The cargo boat is due soon – there's a chance that it might have returned earlier than planned. If it has, and Bob is back but not involved, bring him back here. It would be worth our while to consult him. As an ex-prisoner, he may well have useful information or suggestions as to what we might expect next!'

Peter offered to go and see if the cargo boat had docked and if Big Bob or any of the crew were in his cabin on the other side of the island. The shortest way would be over the mountain, but it was already getting dark and the path was steep and very rocky. It would be safer for Peter to go by the coastal track. He could cycle as far as Sir Wally's, but then the path became rough and narrow with lots of overhanging trees. It would take him a good four hours to get to the wharf and back, but Peter was eager to do what he could to help.

'I'll go right away,' he said.

'Thank you, Peter,' said Sir Wally.

'May I go with him?' asked Geoffrey.

'Certainly not!' said his mother. 'You are staying here with me. I'm not letting you out of my sight!'

'Then at least take Reggie with you, Peter,' said Geoffrey. 'He will be good company. Here,' he added, 'you'd better take the lead, but I expect Reggie will stay close by you. He's very obedient. Even if he does wander off, I'm pretty certain that he'll return to you as soon as you call him back.'

As soon as he saw the lead, Reggie leapt up and eagerly padded after Peter. At the door he looked back at Geoffrey, as if expecting him to come too, but when Geoffrey said, 'Off you go, Reggie. Take care of Peter,' the dog trotted off obediently into the night.

Chapter 24

Peter cycled along the track as far as Sir Wally's cabin with Reggie running along behind him. Beyond the cabin, cycling was no longer an option so Peter left the bike at Sir Wally's cabin and continued on foot, Reggie following him closely.

In the gathering darkness, Peter was very glad to have Reggie's company. There were no cabins along the way and no friendly lights. Peter plodded on in silence for an hour and a half. He was vastly relieved when at last he found himself outside Bob's cabin.

It was all in darkness. He knocked but, as he expected, there was no answer. He walked along to the wharf. A small cruiser was moored there, but no cargo boat.

'Oh dear, Reggie,' said Peter. 'There's no sign of either the cargo boat or Big Bob. There's just a small cruiser, which is probably overnighting here. We'd better get back and tell the others. Come along.'

But Reggie had no intention of coming along! He sniffed the ground and walked on along the shore. Suddenly he barked sharply, as if to attract Peter's attention, and then turned inland and dashed off very determinedly uphill.

He was soon swallowed up in the darkness and, though Peter called and called him, he did not return. After several minutes of calling Reggie in vain, Peter just had to hope that Reggie would find his own way back to The Music Shack.

He turned round and set off back along the path. He knew that he hadn't a hope of finding Reggie in the dark. Perhaps Reggie would get back before he did – and then everyone would think that he, Peter, was lost as well as the children! His best plan was to get back as quickly as possible.

Peter had not gone very far when he heard movement on the path behind him. He turned around and was startled when a black shape leapt upon him. Forgetting that there were no dangerous wild animals on the island, he gasped in terror for a moment. When the animal started licking his face, he realised that it was Reggie.

'Good boy, Reggie! Thank goodness! Am I glad to see you! Come along, let's get back.' He turned back to the path but Reggie, his jaws firmly clamped to the hem of Peter's jacket, was trying to pull him backwards.

'What on earth are you playing at, Reggie? This is no time for games. We must get back to The Music Shack.

Let go of my jacket!'

Reggie had no intention of letting go; he just kept trying to drag Peter backwards. Eventually Peter got the message. Reggie wanted to go in the opposite direction and he wanted Peter to go with him! What possible reason could there be? Was Reggie afraid? Did he find the path too rough? Did he sense danger of some kind?

'What is it, boy?' Peter asked.

Reggie turned to walk away. He went a few steps, then turned and looked back. Peter took a few steps toward him and, as he did so, Reggie turned again and continued walking away, his nose to the ground.

It was then that Peter remembered the lead in his pocket. He took it out and, treading quietly, crept up behind Reggie and grabbed at his collar. But Reggie wasn't going to allow himself to be put on the lead. He wriggled away from Peter's hand and set off uphill.

This made Peter think. Maybe Reggie had walked this way before and knew a way over the mountain path to The Music Shack. If that was the case, Reggie would lead him back there. It would certainly be much shorter and quicker, though more dangerous in the dark, than going back along the coastal route. He could rescue the bike later.

Peter whistled to Reggie and Reggie looked round. Then, tossing his head a little, the dog continued up the mountain track in a very determined way, his nose to the ground. Peter felt quite confident following him.

Up and up they went. The path became both steep and rough, but the moon was well up now and provided quite a bit of light. Peter could see well enough to follow Reggie and avoid the worst of the boulders and stones and prickly gorse, though he had to be cautious.

The rough path followed the course of a stream and Peter could hear tumbling water. The higher they got, the louder the water became. As the path became more rough and treacherous, Peter moved cautiously; a fall from here could be disastrous.

His legs were very tired. He needed to rest for a moment. He sat down on a rock but within seconds Reggie had turned round and was coming back towards him. The dog grabbed Peter's sweater and pulled – there was no time to rest!

Peter got up obediently and started following Reggie again. They were almost at the summit of the hill now, and the noise of tumbling water filled the air. Peter was in a jungle of huge, jagged rocks. Reggie, nose to the ground, was winding his way around them. Suddenly Reggie barked a short sharp bark and disappeared from view.

Peter called and called him but there was no answering bark, no black animal rushing back to him in the moonlight.

Peter sat on a low rock for a while, partly to catch his breath and partly in the hope that Reggie would reappear. He called Reggie again, but there was no sign of him. Peter had no choice but to try to make his own way down the other side of the mountain. Geoffrey would be horrified when he discovered that Reggie was lost, but Peter didn't know what else to do. And maybe Reggie would make his own way home!

First Peter had to find his way through this maze of rocks. Without Reggie's company, he felt very lonely up there on the mountain. He called Reggie once more but still there was no answering bark.

After a challenging trek through boulders and bushes, Peter at last arrived back at The Music Shack with the news that there was no sign of Big Bob and the confession that he had lost Reggie.

The last sighting of the children had been as they headed out to sea; they could be many miles away by now, still at sea, or hidden away on another island. Without any information as to where they might be, and with several hours of darkness ahead, there was little that any of them could do for the moment.

Geoffrey told Peter not to worry too much about Reggie. 'Don't fret, Peter. Reggie is a clever dog. He knows every inch of the island. He'll find his way home for sure.'

For several minutes there was silence in the room – a despondent hopeless silence. It seemed that the children had completely disappeared; captives, last seen heading out to sea. The Quintuckle adults couldn't help thinking that, if a similar situation had arisen back home in England, the police would be out in force by now looking for clues. Here, they felt helpless.

There was little that could be done until daylight. Their only comfort was the thought that it would not be in the kidnappers' interest to harm the children if they were going to demand a ransom.

Chapter 25

Several hours later, Tallulah woke up in the cave behind the waterfall. The roar of water overhead was continuous. She had been dreaming that Amaryllis was wiping her face with a flannel, but she awoke to find that she was not safe at home. Far from it; she was in a cold, gloomy place and she was most certainly not in her bed. But something was wiping her face… Then it all came back to her – the kidnap, the escape, the waterfall!

Some faint light was getting into the cave and she saw that it was not a flannel that was wiping her face, it was an animal's tongue. A wild animal was licking her!

She screamed and put her hand up to protect her face. Reggie barked. It was a dog! It was Reggie – Reggie!

'Oh Reggie!' Tallulah said. 'You clever, clever boy. However did you find us?'

Having woken Tallulah, Reggie leapt onto Gertrude

and Hannibal and soon they were all tumbled together. It was wonderful to see him, a miracle. They felt sure that he would help them somehow. But how? What should they do now? Were their captors still on the mountain looking for them? And what on earth was Reggie doing up here? Did it mean that some of the grown-ups were around? Was it safe to come out of hiding? That was the biggest question of all.

'I don't think we should leave here until we are sure the coast is clear,' said Tallulah. 'The men could easily be lurking on the mountain. They must know that we've hidden among the rocks. They could be quite near, just waiting for us to come out of hiding. We're safe in here.'

'What do you think we should do, then?' asked Hannibal. 'We can't stay here for ever!'

The three children sat for a long moment in silence. They certainly did not want to be captured again, but neither did they want to stay where they were and starve to death! They must make a plan!

Reggie sat and looked at them expectantly. Tallulah stroked him and scratched his head. Reggie loved having his head scratched and he nuzzled her hand. She curled her fingers round his collar – and that's when she had her idea.

'Let's tie my hair ribbon to Reggie's collar, then send him home,' she said. 'He knows the word "home", and he'll go the The Surgery. When Geoffrey sees my hair ribbon, he'll know that Reggie has found us.'

'But how are they going to know where we are? Reggie can't just say, "Follow me. I will find them for you"!' said Hannibal.

'Don't be silly, I know he can't actually say that – though he might do if they give him the chance!'

'Wait a minute,' said Gertrude. 'I've got an idea. Where's that tin of supplies that Geoffrey left here? There are some liquorice rings in it. Let's tie one to the ribbon. That will be a clue for Geoffrey, and he'll know where we are.'

'Good thinking, Gertie. I'll see if I can find the liquorice,' said Hannibal, and groped his way across the cave.

Tallulah untied the remaining ribbon from her hair, threaded the liquorice ring onto it and tied it round Reggie's collar. 'Home, Reggie!' she said. 'Home!'

Reggie sat there looking at each of them in turn.

'Home, Reggie,' said Hannibal.

'Home, Reggie,' said Gertrude.

'Home, Reggie,' said Tallulah.

But Reggie *still* just sat there.

'Home, Reggie,' they all said together, clearly and loudly.

That seemed to persuade Reggie that they really meant it. He got up and moved towards the cave entrance. The children followed him into the space behind the waterfall. They all hugged him in turn, saying, 'Home Reggie!' again.

Reggie gave one farewell wag of his tail and headed for the little space between the rocks. He turned his head to look at them, as if to reassure them that he was on the rescue mission, then squeezed himself between the rocks and disappeared.

The three children felt their way back into the cave. Gertrude picked up the tin of biscuits – there were only four biscuits. They ate one each and Gertrude carefully broke the fourth biscuit into three equal pieces. They ate very slowly, trying to make the biscuits last as long as possible. They washed each mouthful down with fresh water from the waterfall.

As they listened to the rush of water overhead, they wondered how long it would be before a rescue party came. If no rescue party came, when could they dare to venture out? They didn't fall asleep again but huddled together under the blankets for warmth and waited to see what would happen next.

Out on the mountain, Reggie was making his way down through the tangle of rocks and bushes. It was getting light now, and the birds were waking up and beginning to trill and to squawk, but Reggie was on a mission. He ran swiftly without stopping to bark at the birds or to sniff the ground. He had heard the word 'home', and that was where he was going.

When he reached The Surgery, he stood outside the door and barked. There was no response, so he barked again. When there was still no response, he seemed to know exactly what to do. He set off down the track in the direction of The Music Shack and began to bark very loudly as soon as he reached the door.

In the music room, everyone was sitting in absolute silence. They felt so helpless and exhausted. No one had been to bed; no one had slept at all. Everyone was gathered there except for Amaryllis, who had gone into the kitchen to make tea.

When Reggie suddenly started barking loudly outside, they all sat up straight and Peter, who felt so guilty about losing Reggie, raced to the door to let him in. Reggie rushed past him and ran straight to the music room, where he threw himself at Geoffrey and barked an excited greeting.

Geoffrey jumped up and threw his arms around his dog. 'Oh Reggie! Clever boy! You've found your way home. I knew you would. Whatever is this on your collar?' He untied the red hair ribbon and waved it around. 'Anyone recognise this? Did you put it on him, Peter?'

'Not me,' said Peter. 'And he certainly didn't have it when he was out with me. It's very bright. I would certainly have noticed it.'

At that moment Amaryllis came in with a tray of tea. She nearly dropped it when she saw Geoffrey waving the ribbon. 'What are you doing with Tallulah's hair ribbon, Geoffrey? She was wearing it yesterday. Where did you find it?'

'It was tied onto Reggie's collar!'

'Tallulah must have put it on him for fun when they were playing on the beach,' said Quentin.

'No,' said Geoffrey. 'We would have noticed it before, wouldn't we? Tallulah was wearing it yesterday – she must have has tied it on him herself. Don't you see? Tallulah must have tied the ribbon on him and sent him home to let us know. Reggie knows the word "home". He probably went to The Surgery first and then came on here because that's where he last saw me! Oh, clever boy, Reggie!' Geoffrey got down on the floor and hugged Reggie tightly, whilst Reggie licked his face and wagged his tail and barked joyfully. He was so happy to be reunited with his master.

'This is hopeful news at last, but we still don't know where they are,' said Quentin. 'Or whether they are safe.'

'Let's try to sort this out logically,' said Sir Wally. 'If Reggie has been with Tallulah recently, then the children had to have still been on the island when the ribbon was tied on. Since we know that Reggie did not have that ribbon on his collar until fairly recently, the likelihood is that they are still on the island. But we don't know whether they are in the hands of the kidnappers, or whether they have somehow managed to get away and are in hiding somewhere.'

Geoffrey was still holding the ribbon. He pulled off the liquorice ring and stared at it for a moment, then jumped up and started to laugh. Everyone looked him in astonishment. This was certainly not a time for laughter!

'A liquorice ring!' he yelled. 'A liquorice ring! I know where they are. It's all right! I know *exactly* where they are! They are hiding and daren't come out – but we can go and get them. Come on, I'm going right now. Who is coming with me?' He headed for the door.

'But where are we going *to*?' asked Sir Wally.

'Up to the great waterfall,' said Geoffrey. 'I showed them a secret hiding place there. That's where they were when Reggie left them. And I bet that they are still there, too frightened to come out. Maybe the kidnappers are still around.'

'Are you quite sure that you know where they are?' asked Amaryllis.

'I'm absolutely sure. Positive! I keep a little stock of biscuits and sweets up there, including liquorice rings. This is one of them! I just know it is! Come on. What are you waiting for?'

'Just a minute,' said Quentin. 'You think that they dare not come out. If that is so then they must know that there is danger up there. These men might well be armed. Perhaps we should be armed, too.'

'You are right,' said Sir Wally. 'But we have a no-gun policy on the island. However, I think that if we go in sufficient numbers and make a lot of noise there is a good chance that we can drive off the kidnappers. If Geoffrey is right and the children are hiding somewhere and can't come out, then they must fear that their kidnappers are nearby. We must be careful.

'I suggest that we go in two groups then, if necessary, one group can divert the kidnappers while the other group rescues the children. We'll collect Luke and some of the other men on the way. Between us, we will make a lot of noise as we go. Lead the way, Geoffrey.'

'Try not to worry Amaryllis,' said Quentin. 'We'll be fine. We'll be back before you know it.'

'Rubbish, Quentin!' said Amaryllis. 'You don't seriously think that I'm going to stay here, do you? Indeed I am not – I'm coming too. And don't argue,' she added as Quentin opened his mouth to speak. 'Surely you don't think that I am going to sit here doing nothing. Ambrose and Millicent can hold the fort. Just wait for a moment whilst I get some clothes for the children. They must still be in their bathing suits!'

Ambrose and Millicent protested that they didn't want to be left behind, but Amaryllis was adamant. 'We need you to be the welcome party when we get back,' she said. 'You could prepare a meal. The children must be hungry – and we'll be pretty hungry too, after clambering over that mountain!'

Within a few minutes, the search-and-rescue party had set out with Geoffrey and Reggie in the lead to show them the way. They had an arduous climb in front of them, but they were filled with optimism and hope!

Chapter 26

Reggie was always in the lead, moving resolutely and looking behind him frequently to make sure that the others were following him. He was much faster on his four legs than the human party, and he stayed well in front. Sometimes he ran back to the group and pulled at their clothing. 'Hurry up. Hurry up!' he seemed to be saying.

Up they went after him, moving as fast as possible, every now and then stopping to catch their breath. Then Reggie would start to bark, as if to say, 'Come on, you slowcoaches!'

There was no sign of anyone else on the mountain, though they kept a careful watch. But there were plenty of hiding places in the rocks, so they had to stay alert.

At last they heard the roar of the waterfall, distant at first but getting louder all the time. Soon it came into sight and Geoffrey raised his hand as a signal for everyone to stop. The water was thundering over the rocks and they all – except for Geoffrey, of course – wondered where the children could be hiding. And wherever had Reggie disappeared to?

'You wait here,' said Geoffrey. 'I'm not sure that any of you are small enough to follow me. You might get stuck!'

The search party watched as Geoffrey clambered over the huge stones and then, quite suddenly, disappeared from view. They waited anxiously. What would happen next?

In the cave, the three Quintuckle children were huddled together under the blanket. It wasn't as dark as it had been when they had scrambled their way in because daylight was filtering into their hiding place. Dare they venture out, or were the kidnappers still out there looking for them, ready to pounce?

Suddenly, while they were still trying to decide what to do, they heard an excited barking and then Reggie was leaping all over them, his tail wagging furiously. The children jumped up and hugged him – and then Geoffrey appeared.

'Oh, clever Reggie,' said Hannibal. 'You found Geoffrey.'

'And not only me,' said Geoffrey. 'Your parents are here, and Sir Wally and my parents, and Peter. Quite a crowd! Goodness, don't you all look a mess? What ghastly sweaters! Brilliant idea putting the ring of liquorice on the ribbon, by the way. I knew straight away where you were! Come on, let's get out of here.'

The children gladly squeezed out from their hiding place. As they emerged into the light of a sunny day, they were greeted with huge shouts of joy and relief from the rescue party.

Big Bob, from his vantage point across the valley, watched the cavalcade of rescuers struggling up the hillside. He recognised the tall figure of Sir Wally. All would be well now, he thought. Reggie would lead the rescue party to the children's hiding place, wherever that was. It shouldn't be long before the children appeared.

Bob was right. In a very few minutes he saw Reggie reappearing, leading the children out from the rocks. Bob saw the joyous reunion and heard laughter and chatter. He thought about going to join them but decided against it. He would go and see them in the morning. Now he could safely go home. With a light heart, and keeping well out of sight, he made his way down the mountain and headed for his cabin.

Out on the mountain, the children were being bombarded with questions. Everyone was talking at once.

'What happened after you got dragged on to that boat?'
'Was that Big Bob I saw on the boat?'

'What on earth are you wearing? You all look like a walking jumble sale!'

'How did you escape?'

'Did the men talk to you?'

'What did they say?'

'Did they hurt you?'

'Did they threaten you?'

'Let's save all these questions for later,' said Sir Wally. 'We need our energy for the long trek back down the mountain. When we are back at The Music Shack, we'll sit down together and hear the whole story. Now, children, stay close! We don't want any more adventures – and we don't know where those kidnappers are!'

'Don't worry, we'll stick to you like glue,' chorused Hannibal and Gertrude and Tallulah as they set off homewards. No more adventures for them at the moment! What they wanted more than anything else was the safety of The Music Shack and breakfast!

The journey down the mountain was a very merry one. Descending was so much easier than the hard climb up. The children, warmed up by the extra clothes the search party had brought, were exceedingly cheerful. They laughed and chattered as they scrambled down the rough paths.

The grown-ups were vastly relieved to have found the children safe and sound, even if a little bedraggled and very hungry. Now they must get them safely back to The Music Shack, and they must be vigilant; there could still be danger ahead.

But there was absolutely no sign of the kidnappers. Had they left the island? Were they in hiding? Could they be among the rocks and bushes, watching at this very moment? There were plenty of hiding places.

'Let's be optimistic,' said Sir Wally. 'Hopefully they've taken their boat and gone.'

'Perhaps,' said Gertrude. 'But they didn't have a clue where we were. They thought that this island might be somewhere called Zeci. They went off to find someone they knew on the island who would help them – a friend of theirs, apparently. They're probably still looking for him.'

'Zeci is nowhere near here,' said Sir Wally. 'It's miles away. That wasn't very clever of them! They'd obviously been going round in circles which was, as it has turned out, an extremely good thing! But there *is* something which I really don't understand. If that really was Big Bob on the boat, he would most certainly have known where he was. He knows these islands so well. That is a bit of a mystery! Unless...' He paused thoughtfully and didn't finish his sentence.

For the children it was just wonderful to get to The Music Shack, to be greeted by Ambrose and Millicent, who were so relieved and overjoyed to see them. Although they had hardly dared to hope that the children would be found safe and sound, they had tried to take their minds off their dark thoughts by preparing lots of food while the search party was away. After all the activity of the morning, everyone was extremely grateful and tucked enthusiastically into the food. Soon there was nothing left but a few crumbs.

'We won't bother you with too many questions just yet,' said Sir Wally. 'You must be exhausted. But there is one thing in particular that is worrying me, something that I would like to have your opinion on. Do you know whether Big Bob is really implicated in your kidnapping? Geoffrey thinks that he was on that boat.'

'Well,' said Hannibal, 'someone called Bob was definitely one of the kidnappers. We saw him and we heard him. And he was certainly big – absolutely huge, in fact! But we'd never met Big Bob before, so we can't be absolutely sure it's the same man.'

'Yes, someone very big who was called Bob was certainly there,' added Tallulah. 'But I really don't think he wanted to be. I'm almost certain that he saw me when we were looking for somewhere to hide on the mountain, but he sent the other men in the opposite direction. I think that he sent them the wrong way on purpose.'

'That sounds like the sort of thing Big Bob might do. I certainly hope that you are right. I shall indeed be surprised – and very upset – if Big Bob is deeply involved,' said Sir Wally. 'I know for certain that he has often broken the law in the past, but I truly believed that he'd left a life of crime behind him.' He stood up. 'And now I am going to leave you and go back to my cabin. I need some sleep and, from the look of you, I think you all need some sleep, too!'

He was right. One after another, they had begun to drift into sleep: first Hannibal, then Gertrude and Geoffrey succumbed. Tallulah was yawning.

Amaryllis stood up. 'Right, all you sleepyheads. No more talking! We'll all feel better for a few hours' sleep, I think.'

'Yes indeed. Come along, Geoffrey,' said his mother. But Geoffrey was fast asleep already.

'Why not just leave him where he is?' said Amaryllis. 'He looks very comfortable. It would be a shame to wake him up. Let's just put a blanket over him. He'll be fine here. I promise that I'll return him to you when he wakes up.'

Chapter 27

Later that morning, the sleepy household were wakened by a loud knocking on the door of The Music Shack. The only person who was actually up and about was Millicent, who was busy in the kitchen preparing a huge brunch. So loud was the knocking and so startled was Millicent that she dropped the bowl of oranges she was holding, and the oranges rolled around all over the floor. Fortunately they were in a wooden bowl, so at least the floor wasn't covered in broken pottery!'

Millicent abandoned the oranges and went to the door. On the doorstep was a giant of a man and she gasped in astonishment. She had certainly never seen a man quite so big. 'G-good m-morning. C-can I help you?' she stuttered.

'Are the children at home?' asked Big Bob in his big

rumbly voice.

'Yes,' said Millicent, 'but they are still asleep. They were rather late to bed. Can I take a message?'

Big Bob smiled. 'No,' he said. 'Don't wake them. Thank you.' And he turned away.

Millicent called after him. 'Who shall I say called?'

But Big Bob was already walking away with a broad smile on his face. He turned, waved and walked on. He was happy; the children were safe. Now he was off to see Sir Wally. He was going to tell him the whole sorry story and fully confess his part in it. If Sir Wally sent him away from the island, Bob knew that it would be a just punishment, but he fervently hoped that Sir Wally would understand and let him stay in this beautiful place that he now thought of as his home.

He was almost certain that the other kidnappers would not return. They would get into a lot of trouble if they did. They would already be looking elsewhere for new targets for their misdemeanours. By now they would have realised that Bob had changed since they'd all met him in prison, and the best thing for them now would be to keep well clear of Sir Wally's island!

Big Bob strode along the coastal path to Sir Wally's cabin. He wanted to get his conversation with Sir Wally over as quickly as possible. Peter, busy watering the flowers around the door, saw him approaching. 'Hello, Bob,' he said. 'We were half-expecting you to turn up this morning. It seems you had a bit of an adventure! You'd better go in and see Sir Wally right away. You obviously have quite a bit of explaining to do. I'll get Marina to make some coffee.'

Before long, Big Bob was telling Sir Wally the whole story. He had met his old prison companions when he was in Australia buying building materials, and they had asked about life on Hilahila. He had told them about the newly-arrived Quintuckle family and how he was looking forward to the forthcoming concert.

He didn't know about their plans until a few days before he was due to return on the cargo boat. They had turned up with a boat; they said they had bought it but Bob was now fairly certain it was stolen. They said that they wanted to do a bit of sightseeing and sail round the islands, and asked Bob if he would guide them as he knew the area so well. After they had sailed around for a while, they would take him home and drop him off in Hilahila.

They'd argued that it would be more comfortable and more fun than going back on the cargo boat, so Big Bob had agreed. The cargo boat was already loaded, so his work was done, but it would not be leaving for another week. Going with these men meant getting back to the island much earlier, and he was eager to return home to his cabin.

Foolishly, he had set off on the boat with the men. After a few days sailing round the islands, Bob had said that he must return home and asked them to drop him off, but they wanted to sail right round the island first. It was only then that Big Bob discovered their kidnapping plans.

The men thought that they could get a handsome ransom out of Sir Wally by kidnapping the children. Bob wanted nothing to do with any kidnapping, but they turned very nasty and threatened him, even saying that they would kill him and throw him overboard if he wouldn't help.

Bob thought that his best way of helping the children was to try to ensure their escape, so he pretended to go along with the kidnappers' demands. They had left Bob on the boat because they said that they didn't completely trust him, and then had grabbed the children and thrown them into the cabin.

Once they were on the boat and away, Big Bob had done his best to help the children. The kidnappers had done their research and heard that Zeci Island would be deserted; that was their destination. With the children on board, they ordered Bob to guide them to Zeci but instead he had taken them to another island which he knew would be full of people. Later, when the kidnappers thought that he was taking them to Zeci, he had returned them by a roundabout route to Hilahila, to the bay where his own cabin was. He had made up a story about a fictional friend who had a cabin at the top of the hill.

Big Bob stopped talking and looked anxiously at Sir

Wally.

Sir Wally looked back at him solemnly, and then he laughed. 'Don't worry, Bob,' he said. 'I think you have proved yourself to be a totally reformed character. I'm very proud of you, and you can be very proud of yourself. I'm pretty sure that we won't be seeing your former companions again – you know too much about them! My guess is that they will lie low for a bit. They might even reform their ways – though I very much doubt that! However, we'll give them the benefit of the doubt and hope they do. I suggest that we just forget about them and get on with our work here.'

'Right,' said Big Bob. 'Work is the right word, Sir Wally. It's back to the forest for me. It will be a real pleasure to get back to those trees. Trees are much less complicated than people!' He got up from his chair and headed for the door, but it opened and in came Marina with a loaded tray.

'Ah, this is good,' said Sir Wally. 'Marina is obviously not going to let you go without breakfast, and I'm pretty hungry too! Let's eat!'

Chapter 28

A few hours later, everyone in The Music Shack was waking up.

Geoffrey wondered where on earth he was. Certainly he wasn't in his own bed at The Surgery. Whatever was he doing here in The Music Shack? All the adventures of the previous day came flooding back. Had those things really occurred? The kidnap and the search? Could all that have happened in such a short space of time? He must find the other children!

Geoffrey leapt up from the sofa, padded across the room with bare feet and went to look for them. He went to Hannibal's room first. Hannibal was fast asleep but soon woke up when Geoffrey hurled himself onto the bed and shook him. Together they went next door and woke the girls. Soon all the children were heading for the kitchen, where they could hear encouraging sounds of rattling plates and a kettle coming to the boil. They tucked into the scrambled eggs on toast that Millicent had cooked for them and, by the time they'd finished eating, everyone else was awake and gathered round the breakfast table.

'Can we go down to the beach for a while?' asked Hannibal.

'Just for an hour or so,' said Quentin. 'But don't forget that we have a concert and there is still a lot of work to do on *Carnival*. We absolutely *must* rehearse today – unless you think that we should put off the concert for a while. Everyone will understand if you want to leave it for a few weeks. What do you think?'

'No, no!' chorused the children. 'Let's get on with it!'

'We must stick to the date,' said Hannibal.

'Very well,' Quentin said. 'You can have a morning on the beach and this afternoon we'll get down to work in earnest. Okay, everyone?'

'Okay,' they chorused and went off to find their bathers. Before long they were racing down the zigzag path. They stayed on the beach, undisturbed by kidnappers, until the ringing of the big brass bell summoned them back to the house.

After lunch, the family went to the music room for a rehearsal. Amaryllis sat at the piano and everyone else gathered up their instruments. Amaryllis struck an A on the piano, and there was an absolute cacophony of noise as the Quintuckles tuned up.

Suddenly, in a loud voice that could be heard clearly over the noise of the instruments, Geoffrey startled everyone by reciting:

"Elephants are useful friends,
Equipped with handles at both ends.
They have a wrinkled moth-proof hide;
Their teeth are upside down, outside.
If you think the elephant preposterous,
You've probably never seen a rhinosterous."

'My goodness, Geoffrey!' said Quentin. 'And without the book! You *have* been working hard – you know that verse by heart. You don't have to learn them all, you know. You can read them, just like we will read the music on our music stands.'

'I've pretty well learnt them all already,' said Geoffrey. 'They are such fun. But I'll have the book open in front of me, just in case. Mum and Dad are probably getting a bit tired of hearing me spouting the poems, though they say that they are looking forward to the concert.'

'As are many others,' said Quentin. 'So come along, everyone. Let's get on with it! Is everyone tuned up?'

There was a chorus of assent.

'Right, let's get down to work! We don't have a conductor, of course, so keep your eyes on me as much as you can. I'll give you a nod to start you off and try to help with the timing.'

'So much has happened since our last rehearsal,' said Gertrude. 'It certainly seems a very long time ago. What shall we start with?'

'Let's start at the beginning, muddle through to the end without stopping and see how we get on. There are sure to be a few hiccups, but just keep going. After lunch we can start refining. Right, Geoffrey. Introduce us to the lion. Are you ready, Amaryllis and Tallulah?'

Amaryllis nodded, her hands hovering over the piano keys. Tallulah, from her piano, also nodded – though rather nervously.

'The Royal March of the Lion,' declaimed Geoffrey in a loud, clear voice.

"The lion is the king of beasts,
And husband of the lioness.
Gazelles and things on which he feasts
Address him as Your Highoness.
There are those who admire that roar of his,
In the African jungles and veldts,
But I think, wherever a lion is,
I'd rather be somewhere else."

As Geoffrey finished speaking, there was a thunderous knocking at the cabin door. 'Oh dear!' said Quentin. 'What now, I wonder? Hold on, Amaryllis! Go and see who that is, will you, Hannibal? And if you can, get rid of them! We really must get on with this rehearsal.'

Hannibal went to the door. On the doorstep were Sir Wally and a young couple with a baby. Hannibal gazed at them in disbelief. 'Good gracious! Paul! Paul Simmons!' he gasped. 'Is it really you?'

'Yes, it really is me – Good-Gracious-Paul! And this is Sally. And this little bundle is Alice. Are your parents in?'

'Follow me,' said Hannibal. 'You really couldn't have arrived at a better moment. I hope your piano hands are in fine fettle!'

'I'll be off,' said Sir Wally. 'You're in safe hands now. I'll be back to collect you later. Have fun!' And off he went.

As Hannibal opened the door to the music room, Quentin said, 'Come on, Hannibal. We must get going. I hope you managed to get rid of whoever it was!'

'Not exactly!' said Hannibal, as he ushered the newcomers inside.

There was a moment of complete astonished silence and then a hubbub of noise and laughter before Quentin went to the piano and played a crashing chord to bring all the chatter to an end.

'I think we'd like to get you to the piano, Paul. Tallulah will no doubt be delighted to offer you her place!'

Tallulah slid gratefully off the piano stool. Now she could concentrate on her violin.

Amaryllis and Paul, with great verve, plunged into the first chords. There were a few hiccups along the way, but they kept going and, as Quentin had suggested, they muddled through without stopping. They were just playing the last notes as the grandfather clock in the hall struck one.

'Not at all bad,' said Quentin. 'Much better than I had dared to hope. And that is largely thanks to you, Paul! Take the afternoon off, children. Have fun, but don't forget to keep your eyes open for kidnappers – we can't have a concert without you!'

Chapter 29

The week flew by. There were rehearsals every morning, a swim every afternoon and more rehearsals in the evenings.

It was great to have Paul and Sally and little Alice on the island. Paul arrived at The Music Shack early every morning, and Sally and Alice spent most of their time with the dentist's family. The twins and Alice were almost the same age.

The Quintuckles wanted their first concert to be enjoyable for the islanders, so they worked really hard. And suddenly it was Saturday morning, the day of the performance.

Geoffrey and Paul both arrived before the Quintuckles had finished breakfast. The family gathered in the music room to get everything ready. All the chairs had to be put out before the final rehearsal. As soon as they were in place, Quentin disappeared. He came back a few minutes later with his monocycle.

'What on earth are you doing with that?' asked Ambrose.

Quentin grinned. 'I've been asked to give a demonstration of riding it after the concert,' he said. 'Apparently, there are a few people who would like to have a go.'

'Not advisable with no accident and emergency facilities!' said Millicent.

'Don't worry,' said Quentin. 'It'll be fine. I won't let anyone fall off.'

'Well, don't say I didn't warn you!'

There followed a cacophony of tuning up, in the middle of which the door opened and in came Geoffrey.

'Good morning, Geoffrey. Good to see you. Now that everyone is here we can get going,' said Quentin.

The morning flew by and the Quintuckles retired to the kitchen for the sandwiches and fruit juice which Millicent and Amaryllis had prepared.

On the track outside The Music Shack there was already a long queue waiting for the door into the concert room to open. Every single one of the islanders had turned up: Geoffrey's parents, Big Bob and the other woodsmen, the fishermen, the farmers, the clergyman and the shoemakers. Even the new twins, smiling and gurgling, and Sally and Alice.

At the back of the room was a young man sitting with an easel in front of him. He must be Martin, the artist that Sir Wally had mentioned. Was he going to draw the performers as they played? That would be a difficult proposition!

On the platform were the reading desk with the open book upon it, the piano and the xylophone. In came the Quintuckles: Millicent with her clarinet; Ambrose with his trumpet; Quentin with his double bass; Tallulah with her violin; Hannibal with his flute, and Gertrude with her cello. Their entrance was greeted with enthusiastic applause.

They took their places and soon there was a great burst of noise as they tuned up. The audience seemed to enjoy the cacophony and clapped enthusiastically when it came to an end.

In came Geoffrey. The audience fell silent as he took his place at the reading desk and read the introductory poem in a loud voice.

"Camille St. Saëns
Was wracked with pains,
When people addressed him,
As 'Saint Sains'.
He held the human race to blame,
Because it could not pronounce his name.
So he turned with metronome and fife,

To glorify other kinds of life.
Be quiet, please, for here begins
His salute to feathers, furs, and fins."

As he finished, Amaryllis lifted her hands, brought
them down on the piano keys with a crashing first chord
and they were all off on a wild musical gallop. Then it
was Geoffrey's turn again.

"The lion is the king of beasts,
And husband of the lioness.
Gazelles and things on which he feasts
Address him as Your Highoness.
There are those that admire that roar of his,
In the African jungles and veldts,
But I think, wherever a lion is,
I'd rather be somewhere else."

The music for hens and roosters followed, then
tortoises, elephants, donkeys, fossils, each of them
preceded by Geoffrey's reading of the poems. Each one
was rewarded with tumultuous applause. Then came
the swan.

"The swan can swim while sitting down,
For pure conceit he takes the crown.
He looks in the mirror over and over,
And claims to have never heard of Pavlova."

There was a ripple of laughter from the audience, a few notes on the piano and the first notes from the cello. A great hush fell over the audience; the music was so beautiful, and Gertrude's playing so mesmerising, it was as if a spell had been cast. There was a pause of a few seconds after the last notes died away and then a torrent of clapping.

Then came the last poem, the finale.

"Now we've reached the grand finale,
Animale carnivale.
Noises new to sea and land
Issue from the skilful band.
All the strings contort their features,
Imitating crawly creatures.
All the brasses look like mumps
From blowing umpah, umpah, umps.
In outdoing Barnum and Bailey and Ringling,
St. Saëns has done a miraculous thingling."

The Quintuckles plunged into the finale, a wonderful symphony of sound, and the music came to an end. The musicians bowed; their first concert was over. The applause went on for a very long time.

Then followed refreshments for all, and much excited chatter. Everyone wanted to know when the next concert would be. Could they perhaps have a concert every week? Quentin said that he thought that might be a little difficult; perhaps it would be more realistic to have a concert once a month!

Now something happened that delighted the Quintuckles. The islanders had enjoyed themselves so much that they wanted to be a part of this music!

The dentist and his wife – their new twins had behaved beautifully throughout – said that they were both keen singers; they had met when they were members of a choir in Australia. Was there any chance of getting a choir together on the island? Quentin said they should talk to Amaryllis, as she had been in charge of the church choir back in England and had run a school choir as well. Amaryllis thought it a great idea. She announced that she was recruiting for a choir, and in no time at all she had collected twenty-three names. She immediately called a first rehearsal for the following week.

Ralph, who was one of the farmers, said that he'd always wanted to have a go on a xylophone. He was immediately whisked off by Ambrose to have a first lesson right then and there.

Big Bob sought out Millicent and asked if there was any chance that he could try the drum set. He had always had a yearning to be a drummer, he said. 'Come up tomorrow afternoon,' said Millicent. 'We'll have a jam session!'

Quentin rode round the room on his monocycle, to the great enjoyment of the islanders. Lots of them wanted to have a go but Quentin, mindful of Amaryllis's remark about 'no A& E' would not take the risk!

It was some time before the audience finally dispersed and the only people left in The Music Shack were the Quintuckles, Sir Wally, Peter and Marina.

'That was wonderful,' said Sir Wally as he and Peter and Marina prepared to leave. 'Quite wonderful! Far better than I imagined it would be. Thank you. It has certainly given me food for thought, indeed it has! We must have another concert very soon, in a month's time, perhaps? And Amaryllis, could you come and see me in the morning?'

'Yes, of course, Wally. What time shall I come?'

'Oh, any time to suit you.'

'Very well. I'll be there.'

The Quintuckles went to bed happy. The concert had gone very well and all their hard work had paid off.

Amaryllis was thrilled at the thought of forming a choir. Maybe she could even get it to performance standard in time for the next concert!

Chapter 30

On the morning after the concert, the Quintuckle children woke up feeling decidedly flat. After their recent frightening kidnap experience and the excitement and nervous tension of the concert, they were wondering what would happen next.

They couldn't help thinking about their schools in England, which would be on the brink of going back after the summer holidays. A new school year would be starting soon and all their school friends would be back at their desks. The Quintuckles would be on the other side of the world, though none of their friends had the least idea of that!

Would anyone really miss them? Were the police looking for them? What would their teachers think? What would the neighbours think? What about the neighbours who thought that they'd seen them being arrested by the police? What would they say? Or had they already been forgotten? Would the neighbours just shrug their shoulders and say, 'Ah well! What can you expect? That's the Quintuckles for you!'

In the kitchen, the grown-ups were already gathered round the breakfast table. There was an appetising smell of the fresh bread that Millicent had just taken out of the oven. Omelettes were sizzling in the pan.

'Goodness me,' said Amaryllis. 'What long faces! Cheer up. This is the last day of the holidays! School begins tomorrow, so make the most of it!'

'What do you mean?' demanded Gertrude. 'School may be starting in Windleford, but we won't be there!'

'Not in Windleford, perhaps, but you *will* be in school,' said Amaryllis. 'Promptly at 9am tomorrow, lessons will begin in the schoolroom. The summer holidays are over. We've been discussing the timetable, and it's all worked out. Your father will teach History and Geography! I will teach English and French – though heaven knows what sort of an accent you will end up with!

'If you were back in your schools in England – and we certainly hope that we might get back home sometime – you would certainly be studying French. The nearest islands to here are mainly French speaking, so it will be useful to speak the language. Sir Wally is anxious to establish some contact with them, despite the fact that he wants to run this island in his own way.

'Geoffrey's father is going to teach you Biology – as a

doctor he certainly knows the human body well, so you will no doubt become thoroughly familiar with anatomy. And your grandfather is going to attempt to teach you Maths. Despite the fact that he doesn't claim to know much about modern methods of teaching, he says that he was really good at Maths when he was at school, and he's eager to give it a go. You may well find yourselves measuring in rods, poles and perches and weighing in bushels – be warned! However, there are some modern textbooks in the schoolroom that should come in useful!

'Millicent is going to do some cookery with you – yes, including you, Hannibal! Men should be able to cook! Luke will be coming in twice a week to teach Chemistry and Physics. Believe it or not, he actually has a degree in Chemistry so you should be all right there! We're certainly finding out all sorts of surprising facts about the people here.

'School will start promptly at 9am. Geoffrey will be joining us. That means today is the last day of the holidays. I'm off to see Sir Wally. He wants to talk to me about something or other – I have no idea what! Enjoy yourselves – and be good! You're free until the Sunday gathering at six o'clock. Keep a wary eye open for kidnappers!'

They did enjoy the day. Geoffrey joined them soon after breakfast, and they spent the morning on the beach. They kept their eyes open in case the kidnappers returned, even though they were fairly certain that those men would not venture near the island again.

Amaryllis walked to Sir Wally's cabin. She would have been quicker on her bicycle, but she decided that she would enjoy the walk more. She would rather be looking out to the sea and the rocks, or at the trees and flowers, than keeping her eyes fixed on the road with its rough stones and occasional potholes.

She wondered why she had been summoned to see Sir Wally. He had been very insistent that he must see her this morning. The concert had made him think, he said, and they needed to talk.

At Sir Wally's, she was ushered into his study by Marina. 'I'll make the coffee,' she said. 'Oh, by the way, I have a message from Paul and Sally. They are out with Alice, but they'll be back soon. I was told not to let you go until they were back.'

Sir Wally and Amaryllis sat in comfortable armchairs looking out to sea. The view was stupendous. The cabin was perched high on the cliffs overlooking a sandy cove. The blue sky, the blue sea and the golden sand were almost impossibly beautiful, like a photograph in a holiday brochure that looks too good to be true.

'It was a very good concert last night,' said Sir Wally. 'Of course I had been told how good you all were, but I must say that you exceeded all my expectations. It was wonderful. Enlightening and extremely entertaining!'

'I'm so glad about that,' said Amaryllis. 'When you said you wanted to see me this morning, I thought that maybe you were disappointed in some way.'

'No, no,' said Sir Wally. 'Certainly not – quite the opposite, I assure you. I was very impressed with the music. You are a wonderfully talented family, and no doubt the children have had very good teachers. I just wanted to chat about how you are settling in, and how we can work out a good pattern of life for you here on the island, whether you have any particular problems.

'I do understand that life here is very different from Windleford, and I wondered how you feel about it. You seem to have settled in well, and I am sure that you will love it here once you get used to our way of life, but I need to be sure. By the way that cello piece – *The Swan* – that Gertrude played was especially beautiful. That teacher you mentioned would have been proud of her, I'm sure. It was mesmerising!'

'As Gertrude's mother, I may be a little biased, but I do think that she has a very special talent. She does indeed have an amazing teacher – well, that is to say, she *did* have! Gillian Bartholomew is outstanding, and we were delighted when she agreed to teach Gertrude. She takes very few pupils. She is very much in demand as a soloist but she loves teaching – she says that teaching is a good antidote to the stress of the concert platform!

'Quentin takes Gertrude up to London every Thursday after school for her lesson, then he goes off to his choir practice. It works out very well – or I should say it *did* work very well!'

Amaryllis sighed. 'Gillian will wonder what has happened to Gertrude when she doesn't turn up. Lessons start again this week after the summer holidays, and Gertrude has been working so hard.'

'Indeed,' said Sir Wally. 'And are you settling in? I am sorry that there has been such a distressing start to your life here, but I can assure you that those kidnappers will not cause any more trouble. I have made sure of that.'

'Can you be certain?'

'Absolutely certain. They will not return. They have been dealt with! Big Bob will be around, but you certainly have nothing to fear from him. In fact, we have a great deal to thank him for!'

Amaryllis believed him. She was beginning to realise that Sir Wally was an extraordinary man and to be trusted totally, even if he did have some very bizarre ideas. 'Then I will stop worrying,' she said gratefully.

'Good,' said Sir Wally. 'Ah, here comes Marina with the coffee. Paul and Sally are going to be here for the next two weeks, so you will see plenty of them. I'm hoping that you and Paul might give us a little music for two pianos before they go.'

'That will be no problem, I assure you. This evening, perhaps at the Sunday gathering?'

'Excellent.'

That evening most of the islanders gathered in the concert hall for their usual Sunday meeting. Reverend Jack gave a little talk and that was followed by a sing-song with everyone joining in as Amaryllis and Paul hammered away on the two pianos. Afterwards there was tea and cake and island gossip. Yesterday's concert was much praised and everyone was keen to know when the next one would be!

'I think that the next concert should involve the choir,' said Amaryllis, 'so we need to find our singers. We'll have our first choir practice here on Tuesday evening. All those interested, turn up at seven o'clock – the more the merrier. If you know that you'd like to join, you can give me your names now. There are no frightening auditions! If you enjoy singing, just turn up for rehearsals and bring your friends.'

The first person to sign up was Ed, the woodsman. Before the gathering was over, Amaryllis had a number of names for the choir, including that of Big Bob!

Later that day, an unexpected visitor arrived. On the doorstep was a young man with a big roll of paper tucked under his arm. It was Martin, the artist.

The roll of paper turned out to be a painting of all the Quintuckles, plus Geoffrey and Paul, on the stage. Martin had made pencil sketches of them during the concert and had used those to paint the picture. It was a wonderfully vivid painting, so vivid that you would swear that as you looked at it you could hear the music!

'However did you manage to do this so quickly?' asked the Quintuckles.

'I was so excited after the concert that I started

working on it as soon as I got home last night and just kept going until it was finished. It's only a watercolour, just a sketch, really. I'm planning to do a bigger and better version in oils. I brought this to get your opinion.'

'It's great!' the Quintuckles chorused. 'It can go up on the wall in the concert room!'

'No, not this one,' said Martin, rolling up the picture. 'If you are happy with it, I'll get to work on the oils and make a decent frame for it, too. By the way, I hear that you are starting a school. Might you be wanting an art teacher?'

Amaryllis grinned. 'Are you offering?' she asked.

'I most certainly am,' said Martin.

'Then you are hired,' said Amaryllis. 'I think that just about completes our teacher total! Do you have a preference as to which day you would like to come?'

'How about Tuesday afternoon?'

'Tuesday it is,' said Amaryllis, taking a notebook from her pocket and making an entry. 'That completes our timetable, and tomorrow we start. Perfect timing! Thank you.' She turned to the children. 'So, you lot, enjoy the last day of the holidays! But no more adventures for the moment, please!'

Chapter 31

Life on the island for the next few weeks was fairly uneventful. Paul, Sally and Alice went back to England with the promise of returning for Christmas. The Quintuckles settled into a routine: school in the morning, free in the afternoons, music practice and concert rehearsals in the evenings.

There were three weeks before the next concert. The choir would be making their first appearance and would form the first half of the evening's entertainment. Amaryllis was busy with their rehearsals. For the second half, the Quintuckles had decided to perform *Peter and the Wolf*. This was proving to be huge fun, though extremely challenging because they had to adapt it to fit their instruments. Gertrude, playing the cello, would be Peter, and Hannibal's flute would be the bird. Tallulah and her oboe would represent the duck, whilst

Amaryllis and her trombone was the big bad wolf. Millicent on clarinet would be the cat, and also shoot out the rifle shots on her drums, and Ambrose and his trumpet would represent Grandpa. Geoffrey, of course, would be the storyteller.

'You are part of the team now, Geoffrey,' Amaryllis said. 'We couldn't possibly do without you!'

There was still plenty of free time for swimming and rowing and riding. Sir Wally had asked the crew of the cargo boat to bring back balls, tennis racquets and cricket bats to the island so that they could play beach games. Sometimes the children clambered about on the mountain or rode their bikes on the bumpy island tracks – they soon became very experienced menders of punctures!

Often they would go up the mountain and spend time in the secret space beneath the waterfall. Sometimes Luke took them out in the horse and cart and let them each have a turn at holding the reins.

Geoffrey had never realised before what he was missing by not having friends of his own age, but he had certainly not missed out on his education and had been well taught by his parents. As well as teaching him to read and to write, they had given him a good grounding in History and Geography. He knew a great deal about plants and animals and human anatomy, and his tracking skills were phenomenal! He had been quite happy with his life before the arrival of the Quintuckles, but now he was discovering the joys of friendship. He wondered how he had managed before!

But, despite all the fun and the pleasures of the island, the Quintuckle children were missing their schools in England. The summer holidays in England were at an end now. Children would be back at school and the Quintuckles missed their friends and their music lessons and their various activities.

Gertrude was longing to ride her much-loved pony at the stables and to feed him carrots, the treat he loved best. Quentin was missing his football team, and Tallulah was missing her friends and her ballet class. All the Quintuckles were missing the Saturday busking in the square in Windleford. They were, believe it or not, even missing their critical neighbours in Sprinton Avenue!

Being on the island was rather like a holiday that never came to an end. The children were learning that, strange as it may seem, one of the very best things about a holiday is going back home at the end of it feeling refreshed and ready to resume everyday life.

School in the single, well-equipped schoolroom was quite different from school in a big building full of classrooms. It was so much more concentrated, a solid hour and a half of learning, a short break for a drink and a biscuit or bun, then another hour and a half of study.

On Tuesday afternoons Martin came to teach them Art. Unless the weather was bad – this was rare, but sometimes there was a dramatic tropical storm – they held the class outside. Each of the children had a sketchbook. Sometimes Martin asked them to sketch the beach or the forest or the hills, sometimes just a single flower or plant, or maybe sketches of each other.

One day he suggested that they should all go up the mountain to sketch the waterfall. They found it difficult to get the movement of the water in pencil – it was a real challenge but it was fun to try. That day they would have loved to go into their secret space, but they would keep that secret. It had already saved them from disaster once and they might need it again one day!

Sir Wally was a frequent visitor to The Music Shack and took a great interest in all that the Quintuckles were doing. He liked to join in, especially in the art classes. One day he announced that he'd always fancied having a go at portraits and would like to paint each of the Quintuckle children and Geoffrey. He set his easel up in a corner of the concert room and was very secretive about his paintings. He wouldn't let anyone see them – not even Martin – until he had finished all four portraits. After each session, the paintings were carefully locked away in a cupboard and Sir Wally was always careful to put the key in his pocket. He worked on the pictures with great concentration and a broad smile on his face. At last came the day when he finished the portraits.

'Can we see them now?' demanded the children.

'Not yet,' said Sir Wally. 'I've got the portrait painting

bug, and I want to paint *all* the Quintuckles. I would like to paint your parents and grandparents. Then I shall set up an exhibition. We'll have a grand opening and make it a party!'

'I don't think that he's ever going to show us the portraits,' sighed Gertrude. 'I bet they are so awful that he doesn't really want anyone to see them!'

Ambrose was the last member of the Quintuckle clan to be painted by Sir Wally. Early in the morning after this final sitting, Sir Wally arrived in his horse and cart with Luke. The cupboard was unlocked, and all the paintings taken out and loaded into the cart.

'I'm going to finish them in my cabin,' Sir Wally said as he and Luke waved goodbye. 'I'll let you know when they are ready for an exhibition. That will probably be in about two weeks' time.'

The two weeks flew by. One fine sunny morning, there was an unexpected clip-clopping outside The Music Shack. Sir Wally, Peter and Marina had arrived with a pile of canvas wrapped portraits and baskets full of party food and drink. It seemed that the day of the portrait exhibition had come at last!

Hannibal and Gertrude were having a Maths lesson with Ambrose, but when they heard the horse and cart they rushed outside to help unload. Geoffrey and Tallulah were in the forest studying trees and plants with Geoffrey's father, but they returned in time to take the horse to the stables. Betsy and Stanley, who loved the company of other horses, got hugely excited and whinnied and pranced about with delight.

The children went rather reluctantly into the schoolroom to continue the morning's lessons, but it was hard to concentrate. Everyone was wondering about the portraits. What would they be like? Maybe they would be embarrassingly awful and bear no resemblance to the Quintuckles at all!

Halfway through the morning, when they stopped for a break and were having a drink and a biscuit in the kitchen, Peter came in to get some water.

'What are the portraits like, Peter?' asked Gertrude.

'That would be telling,' said Peter. He looked as if he was having difficulty in keeping a straight face as he left the kitchen.

'Oh goodness,' said Tallulah. 'Did you see Peter's face? Those portraits must be awful!'

'Well,' said Amaryllis, 'even if they are, you must be polite about them and pretend that you think they are good. Sir Wally has worked so hard at them. And anyway, what does it matter? This isn't exactly the National Gallery! This art exhibition isn't going to be reviewed in the newspapers!'

At the end of lesson time, the children and Amaryllis joined the others for lunch. Peter and Marina had put all the food out on the garden table. Geoffrey's parents had arrived and the party could begin.

'Do you want to eat first or see the portraits first?' Sir Wally asked.

The reply was unanimous. 'Portraits!' they all shouted.

'Then follow me,' said Sir Wally. He led the way to the door of the concert room, put his hand on the doorknob and waited until everyone was there, then he flung the door open very dramatically and said, 'Enter!'

They all trooped into the concert room. Hannibal was first inside. He stood in the doorway and gasped, then he burst out laughing. The others had to push him forward so that they could see what he found so funny. One by one they got in through the door, saw the portraits and started laughing too.

The pictures were leaning against the walls. They were all life size, instantly recognisable and extremely colourful. The faces were undoubtedly the faces of the Quintuckles and Geoffrey but the bodies were painted as musical instruments – except for Geoffrey's. His body was an open book with little legs and arms attached.

Amaryllis was a graceful dulcimer, Quentin a hugely fat double bass, Ambrose was a gnarled old trumpet, and Millicent an elegant clarinet. Hannibal was a tall thin flute, Gertrude was a cello with the scroll at the top looking like a high curled roll of hair on top of her head. Tallulah was a thin drumstick with the drum itself making a huge crinoline skirt. Paul was there too – he was a fat grand piano. The keys were his teeth and the pedals his feet!

There was a moment of total silence and Sir Wally looked round anxiously at the Quintuckles. 'I hope you're not offended?' he said.

The silence ended in a great burst of laughter.

'Not at all!' gasped Quentin. 'In fact, I think that you have made our concert room complete. When our audiences get tired of listening to the music, they will be able to amuse themselves by gazing round the walls.'

'They are absolutely brilliant,' said Peter. 'The likenesses are truly amazing. I think you have missed out on a career as a cartoonist, Sir Wally!'

'I used to do this sort of thing for the school magazine when I was a boy,' said Sir Wally. 'The art master enjoyed my cartoons. But my headmaster was not at all amused – especially when he saw my drawing of him! I'd turned him into a chimpanzee!'

It was a very merry lunch party. They sat in the sunshine looking at the sea and the sand and the palm trees. Behind them were the mountains with patches of vivid colours where wild flowers were growing.

'If we were on holiday here,' Gertrude whispered to Hannibal, 'this would be absolutely perfect. But don't you think that we would enjoy it even more if we knew that we could go back home when the holiday was over?'

Hannibal nodded. 'Best not to think about that, I suppose,' he said quietly. 'We may have been kidnapped and taken from our home, but at least we are in a lovely

240

place and with nice people! And those nice people saved us when we were kidnapped for a second time! We really can't complain.'

The picnic was over. Everyone had eaten their fill and Sir Wally, Peter and Marina prepared to leave. Sir Wally was going to Australia that afternoon on the cargo boat and would then be taking a plane to London. He had business there but he would be back in a week's time for the concert.

As he was about to leave The Music Shack he asked, 'Is there anything that you would like me to bring from London?'

'Could you bring some spare cello strings?' asked Gertrude.

'And violin strings?' added Tallulah.

'And what about…?' began Quentin.

Sir Wally laughed. 'Just make a list of anything you need and I will get it for you. We certainly don't want strings breaking in the middle of a performance with no replacements available! I will be back the day before the concert. If by any chance I am delayed, please wait until I come back – I most certainly do not want to miss it!'

The Quintuckles made a list of things for Sir Wally to buy and then plunged back into rehearsals. Only two weeks to go now before the concert!

Chapter 32

The days passed very quickly. On Tuesday, Millicent took over the concert room for the evening choir rehearsals. There were twenty-two members, all in good voice and all enjoying themselves hugely. Big Bob and Ed the woodman, both with big bass voices, were in their element.

The whole programme was built around animals, birds and insects; the songs that the choir were singing all made reference to animals. Their programme began with *Nellie the Elephant* and ended with a special arrangement by Millicent of *Old Macdonald Had a Farm*, in which the audience would be invited to join in as the animals. And then, after a short interval, the evening would finish with *Peter and the Wolf*.

Sir Wally arrived back from London in good time and on the morning of the concert Peter rode his bicycle round to The Music Shack with his saddlebag full of the things the Quintuckles had asked Sir Wally to buy. This turned out to be a great blessing because on that very day the mouthpiece on Millicent's clarinet had cracked. Fortunately, a new mouthpiece had been on Sir Wally's list, so all was well. Peter said that two friends of Sir Wally's had returned with him and he would be bringing them to the concert. Could they make sure that there would be chairs for them.

That evening, with the concert due to begin, most of the audience were in their seats. They were looking round at the portraits with huge smiles on their faces. However, there was absolutely no sign of Sir Wally. Then, just as the choir filed in and took their places on the platform, Tallulah spotted Sir Wally and two other people slipping into the back row, though the incoming choir somewhat impeded her view. Good, she thought, the concert could now begin!

The choir sang enthusiastically and surprisingly well. After a raucous rendition of Old *Macdonald*, in which everyone joined with great enthusiasm – though not necessarily with great accuracy – they were rewarded with loud applause and cheers.

There was a brief interval, a short pause for a quick change around of performers. The choir joined the audience, and the Quintuckles and Geoffrey took to the stage. Tallulah picked up her two drumsticks and rattled out a great drumroll to silence everyone for the continuation of the concert.

Peter and the Wolf was greeted with wild enthusiasm. Geoffrey, in his surprisingly clear, loud voice did a great job with the storytelling and the musicians played superbly. After the finale, the Quintuckles stood on the stage, bowing and beaming at the audience.

Sir Wally, clapping wildly, leapt to his feet. So did the man and woman at his side. Gertrude, standing with her cello, suddenly gasped. She turned white – so white that Geoffrey's mother, who was sitting in the front row, thought she was going to faint and rushed towards her.

But Gertrude didn't faint. She just stood there, grasping her cello and staring at the woman at Sir Wally's side. 'Miss Bartholomew!' she gasped. 'It's Miss Bartholomew. It really *is* Miss Bartholomew!' Putting down her cello, she jumped off the platform and hurtled to the back where she threw her arms around the beaming woman.

'Very good, Gertrude,' said Miss Bartholomew. 'Very good indeed. I am proud of you.'

'Yes, indeed,' said the man at her side. 'Very good indeed!' He nodded thoughtfully.

'It was certainly worth coming all this way to hear you,' said Gillian Bartholomew. 'Although my arrival was rather unexpected!'

'I just can't believe that you're here. How did you get here? Did you know that we were here? Ohhhh! Were you *kidnapped*, Miss Bartholomew?'

Gillian Bartholomew glanced at Sir Wally, who merely smiled. 'Kidnapped!' she said. 'Whatever put such an idea into your head, Gertrude?'

'*We* were kidnapped,' said Gertrude, 'so I thought you might have been too!'

'It is certainly true that your disappearance was very sudden – and very strange,' said Miss Bartholomew. 'I was horrified when I read about it in the newspapers – you were all over the newspapers, you know! Your disappearance caused great consternation, I can tell you! You all just seemed to vanish into thin air and no one could find a trace of you. Apparently, your neighbours insisted that you had been arrested, but that was denied by the police. It did sound as though you really had been kidnapped! In answer to your question, I suppose I was *sort* of kidnapped – a gently persuasive sort of kidnapping. And I certainly didn't realise it at the time! I'll tell you all about it later, Gertrude. Oh, by the way, this is Dan Walton.'

'Dan Walton, the conductor?' asked Gertrude.

'Indeed yes, young lady. That's me,' the man said. 'And I'm going to keep an eye on you. I see a concert performer of the future!'

Gertrude blushed. Could this famous conductor really have said that to her!?

'Dan and I will probably be here for a few weeks, but now I think there are lots of other people who want to talk to you – and lots of lovely refreshments too,' said Gillian Bartholomew.

'Where are you staying, Miss Bartholomew?'

'I'm staying with Peter and Marina in the annexe to Wally's house. Dan is in the main cabin with Wally. Shall I come and see you tomorrow?'

Gertrude flung her arms around her teacher. 'Oh yes, yes! And then you can give me a lesson. I'm sure I've fallen into lots of bad habits. I just can't believe that you are really here. I'll probably wake up any minute and find that I've been dreaming! Oh I do so hope that I'm not!'

Chapter 33

When Peter brought Gillian Bartholomew over to The Music Shack in the horse and cart the next morning, she asked the Quintuckles how on earth they had come to be on the island. 'There was such a fuss about you in the papers. So many rumours flying around,' she said. 'But you weren't really kidnapped, were you?'

She was horrified when they told her about the events of that day, how they had been bundled into a trailer in Sprinton Avenue and how terrified they had been.

'I find it hard to believe that Wally could be so cruel,' said Gillian.

Amaryllis explained that Sir Wally hadn't intended the kidnapping to be so brutal.

'He had decided that the island needed musicians and had asked his men to try to find a musical family. He asked them to take a look at us because we had been recommended by someone. He asked them to try to bring us back to settle on the island. But tell us how you came to be here, Miss Bartholomew. Were you kidnapped, too? I still can't believe that you are really here!'

'I wasn't exactly kidnapped – thank goodness. Maybe Wally learnt a lesson from the terrifying way that you were brought here.' Gillian explained how Sir Wally had come to a concert in which she was playing and how, afterwards, he had waited for her at the stage door and invited her to join him for a light supper.

'I wouldn't usually agree to such an invitation from a stranger – that sort of thing quite often happens at the stage door, and I'm quite used to handling a refusal,' said Gillian. 'So I thanked him but politely declined his invitation. Then he told me he was thinking of inviting the conductor as well! I thought he was mad but, at that very moment, Dan came out of the stage door. He saw us talking together and said, "Good heavens, Wally! Is it really you? What on earth are you doing here? I thought you were sunning yourself somewhere in the South Pacific, setting up your own empire." He suggested that we all ate together so Wally could tell him what he was up to.

'And that is what we did. Wally and Dan had known each other from their school days. They were at a boarding school together, in the same house. Before the evening was over, Wally had invited both Dan and me to fly back with him to his island for a short holiday.

Neither of us had any upcoming engagements, so we said yes. To tell you the truth, it all happened so quickly that there was hardly time to think.

'Two days later, we were on our way. We flew first class to Wellington and boarded your island cargo boat – which was quite the opposite of the flight as far as comfort was concerned, but something of an adventure! We arrived on the island yesterday afternoon and were almost immediately whisked off to your concert. What a surprise I had when you walked on stage with your cello, Gertrude! Along with all your family! I was absolutely dumbfounded! And impressed. The concert was of such a very high standard!'

'It's a good job that I didn't see *you*! I would have collapsed with shock!' said Gertrude. 'I wouldn't have been able to play a note! How long are you here for, Miss Bartholomew?'

'I'm not sure. My next engagement is in six weeks' time. I have to be back in good time for that. I haven't had a holiday for a long time, and this certainly seems a great place to stay for a little while. You must show me round the island. We can have some fun together.'

Chapter 34

Gillian Bartholomew's arrival changed everything for the Quintuckles. For the next few days, the children had a great time showing her round the island. Once lessons were done for the day, they scrambled over the hills together and swam in the warm sea, had barbecues on the beach and long walks through the forests. And every evening they enjoyed making music together.

But then, after Gillian had been there for two weeks, there came a day that was different. Gillian had cycled to The Music Shack to give Gertrude a lesson. A sudden and unexpected squall of rain kept them indoors. Instead of going to the beach or the woods, they sat around in the schoolroom. Hannibal was reading a book, and Gertrude, Tallulah and Gillian were playing Scrabble. Tallulah put down the word SCHOOL. As she set the letters out on the board, she sighed.

'I do miss school, especially my friends,' she said. 'I wonder what Miss Watkins is like as a form mistress. I should be in her class now, with Lucy and Amanda.'

'Who are Lucy and Amanda?' asked Gillian.

'They're my very best friends,' Tallulah said. 'At least they were! At the end of last year Miss Hill said, "Oh dear, how I pity poor Miss Watkins. She is going to have to cope with the terrible trio next term." But she laughed when she said it, so I don't think she thought we were all that bad! I suppose that Lucy and Amanda will be known as the terrible *twins* now! And by next year, when they go to the senior school, they will probably have forgotten me altogether.'

'I very much doubt that, Tallulah. You are rather unforgettable! Oh, thank you for that S,' said Gillian as she put down the word CONSIDER. 'That uses all my letters and wins me the game. And now I really have to go. I've been here for ages and Marina will have supper ready soon.'

Gillian was very thoughtful as she cycled back to Sir Wally's cabin. Her final word in the Scrabble game – CONSIDER – had got her thinking. She needed to discuss the Quintuckles with Sir Wally. He needed to consider what was really best for them, she thought. Life on the island was all very well; it was a beautiful place and Gillian was absolutely loving being here. She was sorry that so little time was left before the cargo boat would take her to Australia for her flight home. But for her this was just a holiday, and she was free to travel back home at any time. For young people just starting out in life, Hilahila didn't have much to offer in the way of opportunities. The young Quintuckles would certainly have no chance of making their way in the world of music. She must talk to Wally and try to make him understand that. She would waste no time – she would talk to Wally that very evening!

Chapter 35

A few days later, Sir Wally unexpectedly cycled to The Music Shack. He arrived soon after lessons had finished for the morning. The children had left the schoolroom and were down on the beach.

'Make it a short one,' Millicent had called out as they left. 'Just a quick dip. Lunch will be ready soon.'

A few minutes later, there was a banging of the knocker on the cabin door. Outside, stood Sir Wally.

'Oh hello, Wally!' Millicent said. 'What brings you here? Would you like to stay for lunch?'

'No, thank you, Millicent. Marina is preparing a cliff-top picnic and I shall be in the deepest trouble if I don't get back soon. Could you spare a few moments? And are the others around?'

'Quentin and Amaryllis are still in the schoolroom, I expect, and Ambrose is probably in the stable. The children have gone down to the beach. We could ring the bell for them – that is our rallying signal! The sound carries a long way and if they hear it they will come back, although they will probably be in the sea by now with their ears full of water! They'll be back quite soon I'm sure. I told them that lunch was nearly ready, and they are always hungry!'

'That's fine. It's Quentin and Amaryllis that I really want to speak to first.'

A few minutes later, they were sitting round the kitchen table looking expectantly at Sir Wally. Why was he looking so serious, they wondered?

'I've come to ask you a question,' he said. 'A question that I confess I am somewhat reluctant to ask, but one which I think it is right to ask.'

They all looked puzzled. Had they done something wrong? Had the children misbehaved in some way? They didn't know what to expect – and they certainly didn't expect Sir Wally's question.

'How would you feel about going home?'

They stared at him. What had happened to make Sir Wally ask such a question? And how did he *want* them to answer? For a moment they stared at him in silence, and then they all started speaking at once.

Sir Wally laughed. 'Stop, stop! Let me explain. Gillian has been talking to me – well, she has been doing a little more than talking. She's been telling me off in no uncertain fashion! Gillian thinks that the children should have opportunities that they will not find here, to use their undoubted talents in the wider world. What she actually said is that, much as she likes me and much as she understands what I am trying to do here on the island, I am sadly lacking in wisdom! "Clever, but not practical or wise. Principled, but most definitely a little on the mad side" were her actual words!'

Quentin laughed. 'I think that Gillian puts it beautifully. We all like you, Wally, there is no doubt about that. But I confess that we do think that you are just a little on the mad side – in the nicest possible way, of course! Ah! I hear the children. Shall we tell them why you are here and ask them what they think?'

The children came bursting into the kitchen, shouting and laughing. They fell silent when they saw Sir Wally and the others sitting around the table looking so solemn.

'Sit down,' said Amaryllis. 'Sir Wally has something to say.'

'Have we done something wrong?' asked Tallulah apprehensively.

Sir Wally cleared his throat. 'No, I assure you that you have done nothing wrong,' he said. 'Indeed, it may be *I* who has done something wrong!'

The children stared at him. Whatever did he mean?

'I have a plan for if you want to return to England,' he continued.

The children gasped. This was certainly not what

they were expecting.

Sir Wally continued. 'It goes without saying that should you wish to make the island your permanent home then that would be wonderful. However, a conversation with Gillian has made me do a lot of thinking. I now realise that this island, beautiful as it is, does not offer all the opportunities, particularly those in the field of music, that you might want. Whatever you decide, I want you all to know that The Music Shack is yours, and is available to all or any of you at all times – though the concert hall, with its outside entrance, must always be available to the islanders for events and meetings. You may spend as much time on the island as you like – the more the better – and I will pay all your travel expenses. And your journeys to and from the island will be comfortable in the future, and not at all similar to your arrival here! For which I once more apologise! There will be flights to Australia and then a boat to the island. If you wish to bring friends, that is fine. I will cover the expense. I know that you would only bring people sympathetic to our way of life here.'

He paused. The Quintuckles were all staring at him, hardly believing their ears. 'You don't have to make a decision right now,' he continued. 'Talk it over between yourselves. Gillian and I will come and see you this evening.'

'Lovely,' said Amaryllis. 'Why don't you both come for supper and we'll discuss it then?'

'Thank you, that would be delightful,' said Sir Wally. 'Oh, by the way, if you decide to go you will no doubt want to take your instruments home with you, and probably the monocycle, the tricycle and that old pram, too! If you give me a list, I will buy all the music and musical instruments that you need to keep here so you won't have to carry so much stuff backwards and forwards.'

There was a total silence for a moment and then Hannibal, Gertrude and Tallulah all spoke at once.

'I'd be able to ride Willow again!' said Gertrude, her face lighting up.

'Football on Saturdays!' Hannibal shouted.

'Lucy and Amanda and Tal – the terrible trio!' said Tallulah, grinning widely in anticipation.

'Thank you! We *will* talk it over,' said Quentin. 'But I think you have your answer, Wally.'

'But come for supper tonight anyway,' said Amaryllis.

'Thank you. That would be lovely. And I do have another piece of news, but I will save it until this evening. I'll be off now.'

After Sir Wally had gone, they all started talking and laughing. It was impossible to hear what anyone was saying. Suddenly, there was a shout from Tallulah over the noisy chatter. 'STOP!' she yelled. In the ensuing silence, she said one word: 'Geoffrey!'

The Quintuckles looked at each other.

'We can't leave Geoffrey here alone,' said Tallulah.

The others shook their heads.

'Not possible,' said Hannibal.

'You're right,' said Gertrude. 'We can't leave Geoffrey.'

For a moment there was silence. This changed everything.

The silence was broken by Hannibal. 'Perhaps we could take him with us,' he suggested. 'He could come to my school. Lots of children go to boarding school and then go home for the holidays. It would be just like that, except he'd be boarding with us in Sprinton Avenue.'

'I think that's a great idea, Hann. We'll talk to Tom and Joyce about it,' said Amaryllis. 'They might be very happy for him to have a good schooling in England as long as he is home for the holidays. And I'm sure that Sir Wally would be happy to pay for his flights – he seems to have bottomless pockets! Get on your bike, Hann, and nip over to The Surgery. Ask them all to come round for supper this evening. Don't say anything about us leaving and the possibility of Geoffrey coming back with us, just tell them we have something important to discuss.'

Chapter 36

The supper party that evening was one that none of the children ever forgot. It was quite a squash to get everyone around the table, but nobody minded that.

It was when Millicent brought the pudding in – her very special apple crumble –that Quentin suddenly broke into the noisy chatter and said, 'We are thinking of going back home to Windleford. Sir Wally has agreed.'

There was an immediate silence. Geoffrey and his parents stared at Quentin. Geoffrey sat very still, looking absolutely stricken.

'And we wondered if you would allow us to take Geoffrey with us,' continued Quentin. 'We will be coming back every holiday – Christmas, Easter and in the summer. We would love to have Geoffrey live with us and go to school with Hannibal. We realise that you would miss Geoffrey greatly, but he would be getting a good education and would be here for all of the holidays. Think of it as sending him away to boarding school!' He grinned. 'But with all the home comforts of Sprinton Avenue!' he added.

Geoffrey's look of despair had changed to one of excitement. 'Oh yes,' he said. 'Please, can I go? I'd love to go to proper school!'

Tom and Joyce looked at each other. 'We'll think about it,' said Tom.

'Couldn't you think about it *now*?' asked Geoffrey.

Tom and Joyce laughed. 'Just give us a moment,' said Joyce. 'Let's eat this delicious pudding first!'

Geoffrey had to wait until the end of the meal, then his parents took themselves off to a corner of the room where they sat for what seemed like ages, though it was actually only a few minutes before they returned to the table.

'Yes, Geoffrey,' said Tom. 'You may go if you promise to work hard at your schoolwork.'

'And if you promise to be good – and helpful,' added Joyce with a smile.

'Oh I will – and I do,' said Geoffrey, with a big grin.

'Wonderful,' said Amaryllis. 'And now, Sir Wally, you said that you had some other news for us. Good news, I hope?'

'I'm going to let Gillian tell you,' said Sir Wally. 'Go on, Gillian!'

'Wally and I will be coming back to England with you,'

she said. 'I have a few concert engagements which I must fulfil, and also…' she paused for a moment '…and also, while we are there, Wally and I are going to be married! We may be needing some musicians.'

'Wonderful,' said Quentin. 'Music is indeed the food of love and we will play on!'

'And,' Gillian added, looking thoughtfully at Gertrude and Tallulah, 'I will definitely need some bridesmaids!'

On a Saturday morning a few weeks later, Sprinton Avenue is waking up to a beautiful autumnal day. The Quintuckles have been back for three weeks now. The children are back at school. With Tallulah's return the terrible trio are getting into trouble once more. Gertrude's favourite pony, Willow, is enjoying feasting on carrots, and football is back in Hannibal's life.

Geoffrey is thrilled to be at a real school! Of course he is missing his parents, but he is happy in the knowledge that he will see them at Christmas. He is also looking forward to sharing an island Christmas with the Quintuckles. Should he tell them about the horse-drawn sleigh in which Sir Wally tours the island very early on Christmas morning, throwing presents onto the doorstep of every dwelling? No! He grins to himself. Let them have the fun of finding that out for themselves.

The Windleford Saturday morning routine has been restored. The sun is shining, and the leaves on the trees lining the avenue are turning the most wonderful shades of red and russet. But it is not only the trees that are lining the street: there are people, lots of people, and every single one of them is wreathed in smiles. Not one person is looking disgusted or cross. No one moans about the multicoloured door. Everyone is there, waiting to cheer the Quintuckles on their way to the square.

The Quintuckles are sorting out both themselves and their musical instruments. The bikes, which had been left in the street on the day of the kidnapping, had been put back in their front garden by the bewildered neighbours and were waiting for the Quintuckles on their return. An extra bike has now been added for Geoffrey. The pram, the tricycle, the monocycle and the trailer were delivered to Sprinton Avenue a few days after the Quintuckles arrived home, though none of them have the slightest idea how Sir Wally had got them there! It seems that he is able to manage absolutely anything. In Sprinton Avenue everything is back to normal.

As soon as the Quintuckles have loaded their instruments, they move into the street. Their neighbours cheer – and the cheering is very loud. As the Quintuckles move slowly towards the town centre, the residents of the street fall in behind them and when they arrive at the square, there is already a huge crowd awaiting them. A great cheer goes up as soon as they appear. The policemen are grinning, the children's toes are getting ready to dance.

The Saturday music in the packed square is more popular than ever, and now there is a new attraction. Geoffrey is here to read poems that fit with some of the music. He has an astonishingly loud voice for such a little person – and he is extremely good at persuading people to put money into the collecting bowl!

But the music and readings will not go on for quite so long as usual today. There is a groan from the crowd when the Quintuckles start to pack up their instruments a little earlier than usual. But when Quentin explains that they are required to play at the wedding of very good friends, everyone cheers and puts more money than usual into the collection bowl. 'For the happy couple,' they say.

Quentin doesn't tell them that the happy couple really do not need the money. He simply drops it in at a local charity shop as the family make their way home to get ready for the wedding of Gillian and Wally. The grown-ups are looking forward to it. They are quite confident that the music will play a big part in both the service and the reception party.

But each of the children has a private fear that they don't mention to anyone else! Geoffrey is terrified that he might forget the words of the poem he is going to recite. Although he knows them perfectly well, he decides to keep a copy in his pocket just in case!

Tallulah is worried about her shoes. The white satin bridesmaid shoes are not nearly as comfortable as her everyday shoes! Suppose she were to trip over the train of Gillian's wedding dress when she walks up the aisle? What a disaster that would be!

Hannibal, although he is rather young for the job, is going to be the best man. Suppose he drops the ring – that would be so embarrassing!

And as for Gertrude – well, she worries that her long bridesmaid's dress might get in the way of her cello bow when she is playing *The Swan*, which Sir Wally has specially requested!

Will all be well? They certainly hope so. They are looking forward very much to the reception, when they will be playing some fun music. It won't matter one bit if that all goes a bit wild!

Lightning Source UK Ltd.
Milton Keynes UK
UKHW010657030621
384853UK00001B/38